BAD QUESTIONS

Bad Questions

. A NOVEL .

Len Kruger

Washington Writers' Publishing House
Washington, DC

COVER DESIGN by Andrew Sargas Klein
BOOK DESIGN and TYPOGRAPHY by Barbara Shaw

ISBN 978-1-941551-35-6

Library of Congress Control Number: 2023940457

Printed in the United States of America

WASHINGTON WRITERS' PUBLISHING HOUSE
2814 5th Street NE, #1301
Washington, DC 20017
More information: www.washingtonwriters.org

for Cynthia

Contents

Prologue

I'M NOT A BELIEVER.

I don't believe in numerology or horoscopes or spiritual apparitions twisting our fates. I have no faith in psychics bending spoons or predicting the future. I reject the proposition that we can summon the dead and pester them with questions about the buried past.

Today is the fiftieth anniversary of my father's suicide.

He was a believer. I can sense him within me, just as I can feel the presence of my twelve-and-a-half-year-old self wondering how the universe works, struggling to understand why bad things happen to the good and the not-so-good.

I light my father's yahrzeit, the candle in memory of the dead. It will burn for twenty-four hours in the kitchen sink. My wife doesn't understand—why put it there? You can't be too careful, I always tell her. I make a joke about the imaginary headline in the *Washington Post*: "Woodley Park Man Dies in Fire Set by Memorial Candle."

My father would find that funny. My mother would not.

My father was the believer, my mother the skeptic.

Somewhere, the battle is raging.

. 1 .
Rivulets of Tears

We were the same age—twelve and a half—but Michael Strohman looked like he was sixteen. He wore a beat-up army jacket dotted with protest buttons, and his father was a big-shot anti-war activist. I wore the Jeepers my Mom bought for me at Sears, and my father was a depressed Hebrew school principal.

I knew I wouldn't be the coolest kid in the seventh grade, but I thought I'd be the smartest. Michael Strohman was not only cooler, he was smarter—grasping the concept of geometric proofs before anyone else. Or in my English class, writing what our teacher said was a "masterful" haiku which was supposed to be about "alienation."

Rivulets of tears
Soaking into my parched soul
Eternity, yes!

His haiku got an A, mine an A-minus. Was Michael Strohman's really better than the one I wrote about Denny McLain, the twenty-game loser on the Washington Senators?

Thirty-game winner
The Washington Senators
Twenty-game loser

My haiku was better because it told a story: (1) Denny McLain was great on the Tigers, and (2) then he went to the Senators, and (3) then he stunk. What story did Michael Strohman's haiku tell? And couldn't "parched" be two syllables, thereby breaking the seven-syllable rule? Plus, "eternity" already has four syllables, so all he had to do was think of one more, and he couldn't think of anything better than "yes"?

Michael Strohman first spoke to me during the second week of seventh grade. Starting that summer, I read Agatha Christie murder mysteries, one after the other. I loved trying to figure out who did it and how it was always someone you least suspected. It beat trying to figure out why my father had stayed at home all summer on three-month administrative leave, sitting in his La-Z-Boy with the curtains drawn, while my mom pleaded with him to snap out of it.

I had saved one of the best Agatha Christie mysteries for the beginning of seventh grade: *The Murder of Roger Ackroyd.* By the end of the second week of school, I was halfway through. I was hooked. Who stabbed Roger Ackroyd with the Tunisian dagger in the study? I couldn't figure it out.

Michael Strohman walked up to me in the courtyard during lunch period. He pointed to the book in my hand with his lit cigarette. He smiled.

"The doctor did it," he said.

The doctor. James Sheppard. Country doctor in the small English village of King's Abbot.

"Couldn't be the doctor," I said. "He's the one that tells the story."

"*Think*," Michael said. He tapped his temple. "Are you sure?"

Just like that, *The Murder of Roger Ackroyd* was ruined for me.

How would I ever forget that Dr. James Sheppard was the murderer? Maybe when I was eighty-five, I would forget who did it and I would sit in my wheelchair and finally enjoy *The Murder of Roger Ackroyd.* It would be something to look forward to.

"Thanks a lot," I said, snapping the book shut.

"Sorry, man," he said. "It's for your own good."

"How is it for my own good?"

"I read tons of Agatha Christie mysteries when I was a little kid. They're all the same."

"No, they're not."

"Trust me, after a while you get sick of them. And you think to yourself: do I really care who the killer is?"

"I care."

"No, you don't. Not really."

"Yes, I do. You don't even know me."

He stuck out his hand. "I'm Michael Strohman," he said. "You're in my English class."

"Billy Blumberg," I said, shaking his hand. "I'm in your math class too."

He took a long drag on his cigarette.

"Your haiku about Denny McLain wasn't bad," he said. "Considering."

"Thanks," I said. "Considering what?"

"Considering there are so many more important things to worry about."

"You mean like rivulets of tears?"

He frowned. "No, man. Stuff like society. Injustice. Oppression."

I shrugged. "Yeah, I guess . . ."

"Let me ask you a question. Do you ever wonder where you belong?"

"No."

"You sure about that, Bill-man?"

"I belong right here!" I said. "At Sligo Junior High, Silver Spring, Maryland, United States of America."

He just looked at me.

"Western Hemisphere. Planet Earth," I added.

He tapped his temple again. *Think.*

THE NEXT DAY after school let out, I saw Michael Strohman sitting under a tree, smoking a cigarette. He pointed at me. I pointed to myself. He nodded and motioned me over.

"You busy tomorrow?" he asked.

"Maybe . . ."

Pam Lowenstein walked by, chatting with a couple of her friends. I had known Pam since kindergarten. She had always looked goofy and angular: the red hair, the freckles, the bony elbows. But now she looked different.

"Who's that?" said Michael Strohman.

"Pam Lowenstein. Just some girl in my social studies class."

"You like her?"

"I don't know."

"You should ask her out."

"Yeah, right."

"Why not?"

"She wouldn't go out with me even if we were the last two people on earth. Why don't *you* ask her out?" I said.

"She's way too bourgeois for me."

"I completely agree," I said. I would look up the word "bourgeois" as soon as I got home.

"Look—I didn't bring you over here to talk about Pam Lowenstein." He looked around and lowered his voice. "There's some serious shit going down tomorrow after school."

He told me that his father knew some guy who was the second cousin of one of the Chicago Seven. Tomorrow afternoon this guy was going to lead a "major protest demonstration" in Sligo Park.

"You have to come, Bill-Man. We don't even have a fucking permit. It's gonna be great."

"Why are you inviting me?"

"You've got a brain, man. You know what's really going down, not like most of these idiots around here."

"Thanks!"

I was flattered that Michael Strohman would invite me to anything. But I didn't want to go to a demonstration. I might get tear-gassed or clubbed or some hippie might plant a joint in my pocket and I'd get arrested for drug abuse. Another scandal in the family was the last thing my poor dad needed.

"I wish I could go," I said. "But I can't."

"Why not?"

I had Hebrew school every Monday and Wednesday, 4:15 to 6:00. My mom would drive me there, all the time complaining about my father. My dad would drive me home, usually silent, sometimes sighing when we hit a red light. There was no way out of it.

"Come on. Why can't you go?" he said.

"I, um, got some stupid doctor's appointment."

"Skip it, man. What's more important, the war or your pediatrician giving you a lollipop?"

"It depends on the flavor."

"Huh?"

"I mean, if the lollipop is orange or cherry, the war in Vietnam is more important, but if it's lemon or lime, it's kind of a tie."

He frowned. "Real funny, Bill-man. Seriously, you have to come. The whole world is watching."

"Why do you want me to go so bad?"

"It's called *organizing*."

"What does that mean?"

"It means you have to ditch your doctor's appointment."

I lowered my voice.

"Well, I didn't want to tell you this, but if you have to know—I'm very sick."

He smirked. "You look fine to me."

"I've got a condition." I tried to look like I was about to cry.

He dropped the smirk.

"What's wrong with you?"

I looked around. School had emptied out, with only a few kids walking by. I lowered my voice even more.

"It's very serious. Disease of the duodenum, which is the thing between the stomach and the small intestine . . ."

"I *know* what the duodenum is," he interrupted.

"I really can't talk about it."

"Billy! You're not gonna die on me, are you?"

"Well . . . probably not. But you never know."

He shook his head.

"Remember when I asked if you knew where you belong, and you said you belong right here at this fucking school? It's like, now I know where you're coming from."

"Thanks." I fake-coughed a few times.

"If you end up dying, I'll wear a black armband in your memory."

"Thanks again," I said.

On Thursday, I read in the *Washington Post* about an "unidentified minor, 12" among those arrested in Sligo Creek Park on Wednesday afternoon. On Friday, I saw him in the courtyard during lunch period. He headed straight for me.

"Billy!" He clapped me on the back.

"What was jail like?" I asked.

"It was cool," he said. "I got to make a speech at the demonstration!"

"Really? What did you talk about?"

"I talked about you, man."

"What?"

"You shoulda heard me!" he went on. "I was like, *I want to tell you about my best friend, Billy Blumberg. He wanted to be here, but he was stricken with duodenum cancer.*"

"Actually, I didn't say it was cancer. I said 'disease of the duodenum.'"

"It was great. And then there was this high school chick in the crowd? I think she was starting to, like, cry or something because she felt so bad about your deadly illness."

"Really?"

"Then I said your cancer was like the cancer that's eating away at imperialist American foreign policy in Southeast Asia!"

"That's pretty cool," I said.

He patted my shoulder.

"So, are you gonna be okay?"

"What do you mean?"

"Your doctor's appointment! Are you going to live or what?"

If we were going to be best friends, I needed to tell him the truth.

"Actually . . . ," I looked down at my Jeepers—they were brand new, but already smudged with dirt, "I was kind of lying about being sick and having to go to the doctor's."

"What?"

"Actually, I couldn't go to the demonstration because I had to go to, uh, Hebrew school."

"You shitting me?"

"No."

"Fucking Hebrew school!? That's why you didn't go? You're kidding, right?"

"No."

"Why did you lie to me?"

"I'm sorry."

"Fuck you." He flicked me aside and headed off.

"My dad's the principal!" I called after him. He kept walking.

MICHAEL STROHMAN DIDN'T TALK TO ME for a week. I read more Agatha Christie mysteries—*Cat Among the Pigeons*, *Murder on the Orient Express*, *The ABC Murders*. I was at lunch reading *The Body in the Library*, when I felt somebody looming behind me.

"Still reading that bourgeois crap. Which one are you on now?" he said. I showed him the cover. He rolled his eyes.

"Don't tell me who the murderer is," I said. "Please?"

He sat down across from me.

"Professor Plum in the fucking library with a fucking candlestick."

"Very funny," I said. He stared at me with a weird smile. He smelled like cigarette smoke.

"I'm really sorry about telling you I was gonna die," I said.

He shrugged and reached into his pocket. "Shit, we're all gonna die sooner or later, Bill-Man. I was wondering if you could do me a favor." He pulled out a piece of notebook paper that was folded into eighths, and held it out to me. On the top flap, he had written *Pam L.*

"Pam Lowenstein?" I asked.

He said I was supposed to deliver it to her before fifth-period social studies class.

"Tell her it's from me," he said. "Don't read it."

"I understand," I said, tucking it inside the back cover of my book.

During fourth-period gym class, I couldn't stop thinking about the note. We were suffering through the President's Physical Fitness Test. Today we were doing pull-ups—you had to do ten to "pass" and I couldn't even do one. I jumped up and grabbed the bar, swinging back and forth. I only said I *understood* what he was telling me, not that I wouldn't read it. And what if I lost the note? It was a tiny piece of paper and I lost tiny pieces of paper all the time. If I read it, I could recreate its contents and Michael Strohman or Pam Lowenstein would never know the difference.

"Ready. Set. Go," said my gym teacher, a bald guy with muscles who looked like Mr. Clean. The whole class was watching. After an acceptable five or so seconds of "trying hard," I dropped down.

"Mr. Blumberg . . . GOOSE-EGG!" I heard some snickers.

Today I didn't care. What would the great Michael Strohman write to a girl he was trying to impress? It was probably some sappy love haiku about how he cries tears of joy—*rivulets!*—when he thinks about her. And he probably thought about her all the time. He probably imagined different scenarios where they just happen to meet, you know, accidentally on purpose, and they get along great and become girlfriend and boyfriend.

On the way to fourth period, I stopped at my locker and picked up *The Body in the Library*. I hunched behind the locker door and opened the back of the book where I had stashed the note. My eyes lingered on the last page and I thought I saw who the murderer was. I snapped the book shut. I didn't have much time. Hands shaking, I unfolded the note. It said:

I like you.

That's it? I would have written a much better note. Maybe I would make some joke about our social studies teacher, Mr. Barber, a guy with a buzz cut whose head was shaped like a pumpkin.

I ran up the stairs and into my fifth-period classroom. Pam Lowenstein sat at a desk near the front, talking to some girl sitting next to her. I was nervous. I had hardly spoken to Pam since junior high started, which was weird because we had worked together on a team project in the sixth grade, studying the different systems of the human body. I did the digestive system, making big posters with pictures of stomachs and livers and intestines. As an added touch, I drew dripping bile with a green Magic Marker. *Bile! I like it*, wrote my sixth-grade teacher, Ms. Marvin, on my report.

I stopped at Pam's desk and stood there, out of breath. Now what? Her friend looked at me, eyebrows raised.

"Hi, Billy," Pam said. She seemed happy to see me.

Pam did her project on the reproductive system, but when she made her oral presentation, she got embarrassed and said stuff like "the man's doohickey, goes into the woman's thingamajig." Ms. Marvin got mad and told her to "grow up."

I gave her the note.

"This is from Michael Strohman," I said. "He told me to tell you that he is giving this to you . . ." Pam looked confused.

". . . through me," I added.

"Michael Strohman?" she said.

She read the note and showed it to her friend.

"Wow," said the friend.

"This is *really* from Michael Strohman?" said Pam.

"Yes," I said. "Absolutely."

She stared at the note. Three simple stupid words. *I like you.* That's all it took.

"He said to tell you that you can give me a note back tomorrow and I'll give it to him," I said.

"Okay," Pam said.

The friend's eyes narrowed. "Wait a minute. How do we know this is *really* from Michael Strohman?"

Pam said, "Billy and I are friends." She looked at me and smiled. "I know you wouldn't lie, Billy."

"Thanks!" I said. I liked hearing her say my name. *Billy.*

The next day she gave me a note. *Michael,* it said on the top. It was stapled. I put it in my pocket. I said, "So are you glad to be away from Ms. Marvin?"

"Oh my God, yes!" She turned to her friend. "Our sixth-grade teacher, Ms. Marvin? She was so weird. She once told us that everyone in the class, at one point in their lives, will have their minds snap—and it could be for a few seconds or for the rest of your life."

"Remember the time she read us that Edgar Allan Poe story—'The Masque of the Red Death'?" I said, laughing. "When she got to the part where there's, like, *rivulets* of blood gushing out of people's mouths and noses and eyes?"

"She put the book down," Pam continued, "and started laughing hysterically, like she was crazy!"

"She *was* crazy," I said.

"She was *so* weird," Pam said.

The fifth-period bell rang. This was going really well.

That night, I was able to extract the staple using a bent paper clip. I used a magnifying glass, careful not to tear the paper around the staple holes. Then I re-stapled it with a stapler from my dad's desk. The stapler had a label that said, *Property of Beth Israel Congregation: Do Not Remove From Premises.*

Pam's note to Michael Strohman said: *I like you too!*

MICHAEL STROHMAN AND I had a system. I would deposit Pam's note into the slot in his locker before homeroom. He would slip the response into mine. "Better this way, Bill-man," he said, like he couldn't be bothered talking to me.

I like you a lot, Michael wrote.

I can't believe you like me! Pam wrote back.

Him: *Believe it!*

Her: *I never dreamed you liked me. This is so weird!*

Weird in a good way? he wrote. But instead of the o's in "good" he drew little hearts.

Yes!!!!!! she answered. Six exclamation points.

I talked to Pam every day, for about three or four minutes until the bell rang. I told her what Ms. Marvin had inscribed on the back of my class picture at the end of the year: *To Billy, the fashion plate of the sixth grade.*

"That's kind of weird," Pam said, laughing. "What did your parents say?"

"My dad thought it was funny," I said. "My mom got really mad."

Pam said, "Remember the time Ms. Marvin yelled at me about that thing I had to do on the reproductive system?"

"I don't remember that," I said. "What happened?"

The next morning, on what would be the worst day of my life, I saw that someone had written on my locker with a pencil. It said:

I love you, Billy

My heart was pounding. I didn't recognize the handwriting. But it *had* to be Pam—who else could it possibly be? The writing was shaky and slanted downward from left to right. She must have written it with her left hand to disguise her handwriting. Which could only mean that she knew I was reading her notes and would recognize her handwriting. Which could only mean that she didn't mind I was reading the notes, and in fact, secretly intended the messages in the notes for me.

I rubbed out the message with a pencil eraser. Wasn't *love* a lot better than *like*? How could Michael Strohman compete with someone as clever and charming as myself? I opened the latest note he had left for me in my locker. It said:

Pam: Will U go to the dance w/ me this Sat. night?

Poor Michael Strohman. I almost felt sorry for him.

Pam and her friend were deep in conversation when I came into fifth period, but they stopped talking when they saw me. They smiled at each other. They obviously had been talking about me.

"So . . . ," I said, nervous. "So."

"Do you have something for me?" Pam asked.

"Um, like what?" I asked. Should I have brought a present? Flowers? A box of candy?

"A note, obviously. What do you think?" she said. I handed it over. She read it and showed it to her friend, who squealed in delight. Pam then ripped a blank page out of her loose-leaf notebook and wrote a big *YES!!!* with a felt-tip pen.

"Make sure he gets this," she said, folding it. "*Immediately.*"

But then she said, "You know something, Billy? We think you're the nicest boy in the whole seventh grade."

"Absolutely," said her friend, nodding.

If Pam Lowenstein was in love with me, why was she going to the dance with Michael Strohman? I was the nicest boy in the seventh grade, and didn't that mean—logically—that I was nicer than Michael Strohman? Maybe she had been waiting for me to ask her. But I never did out of respect to Michael Strohman, because loyalty even to someone you hate is the kind of thing one would expect from the nicest boy in the seventh grade.

I thought about it throughout my sixth-period biology class. Should I show up at the dance? Run into her accidentally-on-purpose? And Michael Strohman would see the incredible chemistry between Pam and me and he would back off. How could he not?

The final bell rang. I went to my locker and looked at the eraser smudge marks tracing Pam's message to me. *I love you, Billy.* I picked up my stuff and exited the main building's side entrance, never imagining that this would be the last time I'd ever walk out of Sligo Junior High School.

I planned the rest of my day. I would go up to my room and lock my door. I'd look at the note with my magnifying glass, imagining that same hand—Pam's hand—writing *I love you, Billy* on my locker. Nothing else mattered. She loved me. Billy. And just knowing that would keep my mind strong and unsnapped and happy for the rest of my life.

I stepped onto the pathway that cut through Sligo Creek Park. And it was there I saw them, sitting together under a tree about ten yards off the path. They were sharing a cigarette. Then he kissed her—a real kiss on the lips. I stared at them like it was a TV show and they wouldn't notice.

Pam saw me first. She looked at me, then quickly looked away. But Michael Strohman had no problem looking me right in the eye. He smirked, then pointed to his temple: *Think.*

I crossed the footbridge and chucked my latest Agatha Christie book, *Sparkling Cyanide,* into Sligo Creek. Head down, I kept going, staring at my Jeepers against the blurry gravel path. I couldn't decipher the clues. It was beyond me. How could I possibly know who wrote on my locker and why? How could I have known that I'd see police cars and an ambulance parked in front of my house when I got home? And who could have foreseen—who, indeed—that at the very end of *The Murder of Roger Ackroyd,* Doctor James Sheppard, having been exposed as the murderer, would take his own life?

. 2 .

The Wicked Son

IN MAY OF SIXTH GRADE, our teacher Ms. Marvin showed us how to diagram sentences. She wrote on the blackboard:

I was sick, sick unto death.

"Well??" she said. "Anybody?" We were stumped. What kind of sentence was that?

"Subject! Predicate! Object!" she shouted, whacking the board with the chalk. From behind, her curly red hair shook on her shoulders as she punched the blackboard. She turned around and blasted us with her green-eyed death stare.

"You must know this or you will be lost, at sea, *doomed*, when you go to junior high," she said, giving us her creepy smile. "If you make it to junior high."

She placed the chalk—delicately—in the chalk holder.

"I want to tell you people something. You may think that life is a bowl of cherries and that you can control everything that happens to you. But you can't."

We had heard this before. "There are forces out there," she went on. "Forces we can't hear or see or smell or taste. Do they control our destinies? Well, maybe they do."

Ms. Marvin always talked about "forces" in the world beyond and how you were blind if you couldn't recognize them even though they were invisible. That never made sense to me. I looked at my desktop. I had converted all the curse words: *Fuck – Book. Cock – Cook. Prick – Brick.* I heard a page rustle, a pencil roll on a desk. I couldn't wait until summer vacation started.

"News flash!" Ms. Marvin was staring at me, her eyes blazing. "At some point in your lives, your minds will snap. All of you. Do you understand? Snap. Crackle. Pop!"

She grinned.

"You—each and every one of you—will enter the Kingdom of Madness. It may be for the briefest of seconds. It may be for a week. It may be for a year. And it may be for the rest of your lives. But it will happen. It will happen when you least expect it. And there's not a thing you can do about it."

This, I hadn't heard before. Would *my* mind snap, I wondered? When? Where? What if it happened when I grew up and I was driving a car or operating heavy machinery? And if it happened—or according to Ms. Marvin, *when* it happened—would my mind snap for "the briefest of seconds" or for fifty years?

And . . . was this what was happening to my dad?

The previous week, he had woken up and decided he didn't want to go to work. "I can't bear it," he said over and over, sitting at the kitchen table, crunching on his Cheerios. He ate them dry, without milk.

There was only a month left of school. "Just stick it out 'til this summer," my mother said. "Talk to the president of the congregation. Talk to the rabbi."

"I don't want to bother them. They have their own problems."

"Yes, Murray. And now they have another problem."

He crunched on another mouthful of Cheerios.

"Talk to them, Murray."

"They can't do anything."

"How do you know?"

"I just know. What's the use?"

"Maybe you should see somebody."

"No," he said. He glanced at me for a second, then looked back toward my mother. "I'd have to drive downtown, find a place to park. All that traffic. It's too much trouble."

"They have doctors in Silver Spring, Murray."

"I don't want to fool with it."

"So what are you going to do? Sit at home all day?"

"Just for a while."

"Great. And will your employers stop paying your salary for a while? Will we stop paying our mortgage for a while? Will we stop eating for a while?"

"Maybe you could talk to the rabbi."

"Sure. And what do I tell him?"

"Tell him," he said, his voice choked, "I can't bear it." He stood up and walked out of the kitchen, head down.

"Your father has a 'condition,'" my mother told me. She looked worried. I wondered if it was possible that I had a condition too. Every morning, Monday through Friday, I woke up and didn't want to go to school either. Perhaps we were entering the Kingdom of Madness together, like the three-legged sack race at some father and son picnic.

The synagogue placed him on sick leave through the summer, with the agreement that he'd visit a psychiatrist and come back to work in the fall. After a month of putting it off, he made an appointment with a doctor in Rockville, someone recommended by the rabbi. The morning of his appointment he was grim.

"I feel like I have an appointment with the hangman," he said, twisting a spoon in his oatmeal. "At the gallows," he added. "In Rockville."

"I can't listen to this," my mother said. She stood up and left.

We sat there in silence, me and my father. He stared into his oatmeal.

"Maybe the governor will commute your sentence?" I said, finally.

He looked at me, smiling a little.

"Ah, but who—in this particular case—is the governor?"

"Marvin Mandel?" I said. Mandel was the governor of Maryland, the guy who succeeded Spiro Agnew.

"Separation of church and state. He doesn't get involved in affairs of the religious community."

"Maybe the rabbi is the governor?" I suggested. "He'll call and say you don't have to go."

"Impossible. He's the one who wants me to go in the first place."

He took another spoonful of oatmeal. He didn't put milk in that either.

"Who else?" he said.

"The head of the Jewish Theological Seminary?"

"What does the head of the Jewish Theological Seminary care about some nobody Hebrew school principal in Silver Spring, Maryland?"

"The Prime Minister of Israel?"

"God knows, he's got plenty of his own troubles."

"Sammy Davis Jr.?"

"A convert. Not that there's anything wrong with that."

"Captain Kirk?"

"Who?"

"This kid in my Hebrew school class told me William Shatner is Jewish."

He sighed, long and hard.

"Wonderful. So my fate would rest in the hands of a spaceman who wears gold pajamas and runs around firing ray guns at some poor schnook in a rubber lizard suit? It's hopeless."

I tried to think of something to say.

"What about God?"

He patted me on the shoulder. "What *about* God?"

My father said that he turned right when he should have turned left on Rockville Pike. He missed his appointment and then he went to lunch at the Tastee Diner and then he headed home. When he returned, he seemed happier than he had been in a long time. He took it as a sign that he wasn't meant to go to a psychiatrist and sit there and talk about, as he put it, "problems that no one really wants to be bothered with anyway, even if you're paying them to hear it."

"That's his job, Murray." My mother looked like she was going to strangle him. He flipped his car keys onto the kitchen counter.

"I have no doubt that turning the wrong way on Rockville Pike was a gift from the Almighty."

"Some gift. So what exactly is your next step in this process?"

He sat down at the kitchen table. He winked at me.

"And not just a gift to me!" he explained. "God gave this man, this psychiatrist, one of the most precious gifts we can receive in this life. An unanticipated and spontaneous hour of freedom. Isn't that a good thing?"

"What do you mean?" I asked.

"Be quiet, Billy," my mother said. "Don't encourage him."

He ignored her. "Think about it! This doctor's sitting in his office. He looks at the clock. 11:00. He's thinking: Ugh, a new patient, with all sorts of craziness I'll have to fool with. But then it's 11:05, 11:10, 11:15. The joy is building in his heart. He can read the paper, listen to the radio, maybe eat a sandwich. Granted, it would be somewhat of an early lunch. But the departure from his usual routine is what makes it such a blessing."

"It's like if I found out that I didn't have to go to Hebrew school next year," I said. "The joy would be building in my heart."

"Exactly!" my father said.

Usually when I said I hated Hebrew school, he would tell me it was an experience I would "treasure" when I grew up. When that didn't work, he would talk about the position he was in and ask how it would look if the principal's son dropped out. But now, it was: "Exactly!" Maybe—I hoped—as part of his mind snapping, I wouldn't have to go back to Hebrew school when seventh grade started.

But I did have to go back. We both did. By the end of the summer, despite never going to the psychiatrist, my father seemed a lot better. My mother convinced the rabbi and the synagogue board to let him return.

Seventh grade started. There were twenty-five kids in my Hebrew school class and none of us wanted to be there. Hadn't we already spent the whole day being tortured in junior high school? How much more could we take?

Mr. Katz was our seventh-grade Hebrew school teacher. We referred to him as "Young Mr. Katz" because there were two of them, father and son, both Israelis. "Old Mr. Katz" was about eighty, and kids were pretty nice to him because he had the shakes and reminded everybody of their grandfathers. Young Mr. Katz was another story.

"You are animals of the zoo!" he would shout as kids punched each other, shouted, ran around. We laughed at his bad English. Young Mr. Katz had been in the Israeli army and rumor had it that he was so afraid of getting shot or blown up that he'd deserted on Day Five of the Six Day War. He trekked in the Negev desert for forty days and forty nights, not knowing the war was over. He had two choices: either he could surrender to the Egyptians or he could come to work for my dad in Silver Spring and teach Hebrew school.

"Don't play the fool, fool!" Anyone who could make him say this earned points, although it was never decided what the points were good for.

THE WEATHER WAS BEAUTIFUL on the day of the protest demonstration that Michael Strohman had invited me to. It was one of those crisp September days, cool and sunny, with a nice breeze rustling the leaves. And there we were, cooped up behind white cinder-block walls and tiny windows, listening to Young Mr. Katz lecture us on the destruction of the Second Temple.

There wasn't much listening. I sat at my desk quietly watching the escalating chaos swirling around me.

"No, no, no!" yelled Young Mr. Katz.

"Yes, yes, yes!" said Lawrence Feinbaum, as he danced around the room. His father was the president of the congregation. He didn't worry about embarrassing his dad.

An empty chair tipped over. A copy of *History of World Jewry, Part 2* fell on the floor with a loud bang. Laughter. Many copies of *History of World Jewry, Part 2* fell on the floor, the bangs perfectly synchronized. More laughter. Howling laughter. We were animals of the zoo. Feinbaum had a paper airplane. He had drawn little Jewish stars on the wings, like it was a jet fighter in the Israeli air force. Young Mr. Katz pointed at him.

"No!" he thundered.

"Throw it! Throw it!" sang a bunch of Feinbaum's friends.

I looked out the window. I could have been at that anti-war demonstration in Sligo Park with Michael Strohman. There would have been cool music, interesting people. Maybe I would have smoked a joint for the first time. I was a little bit scared of getting high, but it had to be better than this.

Feinbaum cocked his arm, taking aim. I looked down at my desk. Someone had written *Pussy*. I changed it to *Bossy*.

The classroom door flew open and in came my father. He surveyed the room, blinking.

"Freeze," he said. He never raised his voice. He looked around the room, from face to face, a few seconds each. Nobody moved. This was his famous Look, where he stared into the soul of each child, then turned away, shaking his head in sorrow and disappointment. I'd heard him brag about it to my mother. He said he could transform a roomful of unruly children—"a mob with no sense of collective responsibility"—into a group of trembling children who felt "shame and remorse over their actions." He said that it was like casting a spell of peace and righteousness, that if The Look could somehow be applied on the world stage, "the lion might one day lie down with the lamb."

He was halfway through the room with The Look. Next would come The Speech telling us our behavior was a disgrace to our families, our community, and to the Jewish People in general. But before my dad could get to The Speech, Young Mr. Katz had to show everybody who was boss.

"You fly this, you fly out!" he shouted at Feinbaum, who, frozen in place, still had the paper airplane ready to launch.

A few titters rippled through the room. Feinbaum shrugged, then let it fly. The paper airplane darted toward Young Mr. Katz, dipped downward, swooped upward, then veered toward my father. It hit him on the head, right under the rim of his yarmulke. What were the odds that a paper airplane could hit his head at such a crazy angle? A million to one? A billion to one?

The yarmulke popped off his head.

"No!" cried Young Mr. Katz. There was a moment of stunned silence. Then the room erupted in laughter. My father rubbed his head. His eyes darted, confused, like he was cornered. The spell was broken and the lambs were mauling the lion.

I laughed too. And why not? Didn't my dad force me to go to this stupid Hebrew school class and wasn't it a boring waste of time that all the cool kids in junior high—like Michael Strohman—didn't have to put up with? Didn't I deserve a good laugh just as much as anybody else?

And it was then, as I was laughing, that my father gave me a look—and it was no fake Look.

Even you? his eyes said, boring into me. Then he looked away.

It was the same face he had last spring at the breakfast table, crunching on those dry Cheerios when he couldn't bear it anymore. He put his head down and walked out, leaving the yarmulke lying on the floor, like a dead animal. Everybody was still laughing. I looked down and the words on the desk were blurry.

After class we drove home. *Oh, by the way*, I had planned to say as I pulled my car door shut and snapped on my seat belt, *sorry about the laughing*. But he wouldn't look me in the eye. I didn't think he wanted me to say anything.

We were almost home, driving down Sligo Parkway, when he broke the silence.

"When you learn how to drive," he said in his soft, patient voice, "it is important to be a defensive driver. Do you know what that means? Assume the worst thing that can happen and be ready for it."

He loved to talk about traffic stuff—how you should plan your lane in advance, avoid the tricky intersections.

"What's the worst thing that can happen?" I asked, relieved that we were having a regular old conversation.

"What if the driver in front of me slams on his brakes with no warning? What if oncoming traffic careens into my lane? What if the guy behind me is drunk? You have to be ready. Never relax behind the wheel. Never let your guard down."

"Yeah but," I chuckled, "what if . . . a meteor comes crashing down? Or what if there's an earthquake and the car falls into one of those big cracks in the ground and the car keeps falling and falling until it reaches the earth's core?"

He should have asked me, with his little laugh, what the odds were of *that* happening. But he just let out a little sigh and lapsed back into the awful silence.

We stopped at a traffic light. I rolled down the window. The crickets chirped, the car idled.

"Don't play the fool, fool," I heard Young Mr. Katz say, softly, sadly, somewhere far away.

IN THE JEWISH TRADITION it is customary after a person dies to invite people to the house. Someone orders big platters of food, and family and friends are supposed to comfort you. My mother loved to be comforted, even by people she couldn't stand. Even Harold Feinbaum, the president of the congregation, who my

father feared and hated, who my mother commonly referred to as "that bastard, that son of a bitch." He walked into our family room in the basement and my mother started crying and he put his arms around her and she put her arms around him. *Thank you for everything, Harold,* she said.

I didn't feel like talking to anybody. People would see me and smile sadly. *I'm so sorry*, they would say, *how are you, Billy? Thanks*, I'd say, staring at the ground. *Fine*, I'd grunt, expressionless. Then they would go away.

I stood next to the fish platter: nova, sable, and baked kippered salmon surrounding a whole white fish, its sides picked clean by white plastic forks. I looked at the dead fish eye. Wasn't it obvious that I wasn't laughing *at* him, I was laughing *with* him? That if he could have seen himself, he would agree that *any* yarmulke hopping off *anyone's* head looked pretty hilarious. It was like something out of a cartoon—and wouldn't he have loved a cartoon about yarmulkes catapulting off people's heads because they could only make a cartoon like that in Israel, and wasn't it a miracle that only in the Land of Israel would Jewish cartoonists make a cartoon for Jewish children about yarmulkes rocketing off Hebrew school principals' heads, shooting through the stratosphere, orbiting the earth for forty days and forty nights, then reentering the atmosphere where the yarmulke splashes down in the Red Sea, recovered by frogmen in slippery black rubber suits? Hilarious! Wouldn't my father have loved that? Wouldn't he have laughed at that? No. Just because I hated Hebrew school and wanted to be like Michael Strohman didn't mean I should have laughed at him when the yarmulke flew off his head. What was wrong with me? I thought about the Passover story of the Four Sons, how each ask a question about the Passover Seder, and how that question lays bare their natures for all to see. Which son was I? I was the Wicked Son, the one who asks his father: What is all this boring crap you make me do every year? Extra bonus question: Why does this night *have* to be different from all other nights?

"Hi, Billy."

I looked up from the fish. I couldn't believe it. Ms. Marvin, my former teacher, stood in front of me. I hadn't seen her since the end of sixth grade.

"What are you doing here?" I said.

"I saw the obituary," she said. "I'm so sorry."

That figured. Ms. Marvin loved obituaries. Once she gave us an assignment to make up our own. Kids wrote about being famous baseball players, movie stars, presidents of the United States. Everyone lived to be one hundred and had swimming pools in their backyards.

In my obituary, I wrote that on April 23, my twelfth birthday, I was hit in the head by a foul ball at a Senators game. My brain spontaneously rearranged itself so that I became a genius—such a genius, in fact, that I was able to go to Harvard after the sixth grade instead of going to junior high. Harvard was a lot better than junior high because you didn't have to take gym. After I graduated with a PhD in nuclear physics, I invented flying cars, like the ones they had on *The Jetsons*. I became a billionaire and bought the Washington Senators baseball team. As the owner, I decreed that every April 23 I would get to play first base for one inning. On my one hundredth birthday, I was struck on the head by a line drive hit by Mickey Mantle's great-grandson. I died peacefully in the dugout. The end.

Ms. Marvin gave me a B-minus. *Where is the heartbreak?* she wrote, *where is the tragedy?*

Now I could write an A-plus obituary about how my father

died when I was in the seventh grade. I looked at Ms. Marvin, with her floppy red hair and freckled face nodding sadly in my direction. Why was she here?

"How are you doing, Billy?"

"Fine."

"Are you doing okay?"

"I guess."

"Are you sure?"

"Yeah."

I looked around. Across the room, next to the folded-up ping-pong table, my mother was talking to Young Mr. Katz. Her eyes darted, searching for an escape route.

"So. How's junior high?" Ms. Marvin asked.

"Fine."

"I miss you in my class, you know."

"Thanks."

"I just wanted to come and tell you how sorry I am about your dad."

"Thanks."

"He was a very nice man. I met him at a parent–teacher meeting."

"Right." I remembered that. My mother was annoyed because Ms. Marvin had said that I was quiet—"too quiet"—and made some dumb joke that it was the quiet ones you have to watch out for. My father said she seemed like a nice enough woman, and that as an education professional you had to joke around like that or you went crazy.

"He seemed to be in very good health," said Ms. Marvin.

"Yeah," I said. "I guess."

"His passing was such a shock."

My mother had moved on to Old Mr. Katz. His hand shook

badly as he patted her on the shoulder. I wondered if his hands shook all the time, even when he was sleeping.

"What happened?" asked Ms. Marvin.

"I'm not allowed to talk about it," I said.

"Trust me when I say that talking about horrible things makes you feel better. Believe me, I know."

She leaned closer toward me. I could smell her perfume. "You know, Billy, now that I'm not your teacher anymore, we can be friends."

I didn't know what to say. Why would I want to be friends with Ms. Marvin? It would be like becoming friends with the mailman or my dentist.

"And now that we're friends," she said, "I can tell you something I never would have told you when I was your teacher."

"Okay."

"I've taught a lot of kids over the past seven years. You're one of my all-time favorite students."

"Thanks," I said.

"Do you want to know why I consider you one of my all-time favorites?"

"I guess."

"It's because you're charmingly weird. You have quirks. I like that."

"I'm not weird," I said.

"Yes, you are. It's a good thing, not to be like everybody else. Trust me, I'm weird too."

If she liked me so much—her fellow weirdo—why did she give me two C's on my final report card? The C in handwriting I could understand, because my handwriting was horrible. But science? Fifty percent of our grade was based on our science fair project. I carved a riverbed into a block of clay to illustrate the

"Principles of Erosion." My father offered to help, but I refused because Ms. Marvin made us promise not to let parents do our projects for us.

"You're sure?" my father asked. "I know how this science fair business works. It has nothing to do with science. It's all about who can paint the prettiest picture."

"I'm like the worst artist in the world," I said.

"Exactly. Trust me, all of your classmates' parents will spend valuable leisure time working on these fakakta projects. You're sure you don't want me to help?"

Billy: C-minus. I expected so much more from you, Ms. Marvin wrote on the enormous poster board with the horrible handwriting that accompanied my small grayish-greenish block of clay. What did she expect from me?

She looked around the room. Clumps of people spoke in hushed tones. My mother was looking at us, her brow furrowed, while she talked to the rabbi.

"So what's all this called?" Ms. Marvin said, making a grand sweeping gesture with her arm.

"Sitting shiva."

"It's nice. Kind of like an Irish wake, except no booze."

She surveyed the fish platter. "Look at all this food! Now what's this?" she asked, pointing at a gray blob glistening with clear jelly.

"It's called gefilte fish."

"What does gefilte mean?"

"I don't really know."

"Well, what kind of fish is in it?"

"I'm really not sure."

She poked at a piece with her finger.

"It's kind of like a cold slimy fish hamburger."

"Why don't you try it?" I speared a gefilte fish ball with a blue plastic toothpick.

She hesitated.

"You have to put this on it first," I said. I dunked the fish ball into a bowl of white horseradish. The plastic toothpick was shaped like a sword, with a flat blade and a little sword handle. I twisted it around and around, layering the gefilte fish ball with great gobs of white-hot horseradish. She would swallow it and her eyes would bug out and she'd start gagging. Maybe then she'd go away.

"Here," I said, handing it to her, like it was nothing.

She shrugged and popped the whole thing into her mouth. A muscle in her face twitched.

"Not bad," she said, nodding. "I think I'll take another, if you don't mind."

She never got the chance. My mother was at my elbow, glaring at Ms. Marvin.

"Excuse me. Are you who I think you are?"

"Yes, Ms. Blumberg, I'm Nancy Marvin, Billy's sixth-grade teacher. I just wanted to say . . ."

"I know who you are."

"I just wanted to say how sorry I am about your husband."

"Well, maybe you should tell me how sorry you are for making fun of my son's clothing."

"Excuse me?"

"You don't remember? Let me refresh your memory. You wrote that he was 'the fashion plate of the sixth grade' on the back of his class picture."

"I'm sorry. It was a joke."

"Do you think it's easy? Do you have children of your own, *Ms.* Marvin?"

"No."

"Are you married?"

"No."

"So you don't know, do you? You don't know what it's like to pick out clothes for a husband, may he rest in peace, who's so depressed he doesn't care if his suits have holes in them. You don't know what it's like to outfit a twelve-year-old boy who would be perfectly happy to dress like a beggar if I left it up to him."

"No, Ms. Blumberg," she said. "I don't know what it's like."

"And you come into my house on the worst day of my life! I don't even know you! What are you doing here?"

"I should go," Ms. Marvin said, looking at me.

My mother turned to me. "And you! Standing here having a pleasant little chat with this crazy woman? What's the matter with you? Don't you have any sense?"

I closed my eyes.

Fuck – Book.

Cock – Cook.

Prick – Brick.

My mother let out a few shrieking sobs. The rabbi came over to comfort her.

"Do you see what my poor husband had to put up with?" she cried out.

I was sick, sick unto death.

I opened my eyes. Everybody was looking.

Ms. Marvin gathered up her pocketbook. She leaned close to my face, like she was going to tell me something. I could smell the gefilte fish on her breath, the white horseradish I made her eat. I wanted to gag and vomit and run screaming from the room and never come back.

"It's not your fault," she whispered.

. 3 .

What Is the Law?

"WHY DO WE HAVE TO MOVE?" I asked my mother. "I don't know anybody in Rockville."

"That's the point," she said. We could start fresh after the accident, which was how she referred to it, always. The accident. Plus, Rockville was near her new job in Potomac. And we certainly couldn't afford to live in Potomac, she told me, as if it was my fault. We moved quickly—three weeks. "Thank God we rent and our lease is up," my mom said. "Perfect timing."

The kids in my new school would want to know why we moved. What would I say? That termites had invaded us in Silver Spring and the whole house was condemned? How one night I was sleeping and I heard this rumbling and cracking down below, the sound of wood popping and splitting. And then—the house buckled and shook like an earthquake or an explosion and the next thing I knew, my bed and bedroom had fallen through the floor and were now in the basement. So we had to move. Immediately. It was on Channel 9 Eyewitness News. Hadn't they seen it?

On the first day at my new school, West Montgomery Junior High, I had to meet with Mr. Wilson, the seventh-grade guidance counselor. Mr. Wilson had a white beard, white shirt, red tie, and suspenders. He looked like Santa Claus if Santa Claus sat around with his coat off, drinking thick black coffee out of an off-white stained coffee mug that said *Virginia is for Lovers.*

Mr. Wilson was jolly, too. "Nice to meet you!" he said, shaking my hand and squeezing too hard. He motioned to a chair facing his desk. I sat. I could hear a mimeograph machine clacking away in another room.

"Question!" he proclaimed, grinning. "There's two kinds of people in this world. One gets up in the morning and says, 'Good morning, God.' The other gets up and says, 'Oh God, it's morning.' Which one are you?"

"Um, I don't know." I thought for a second. "Good morning, God."

"Great!" he said, opening a manila folder on his desk. "Let's take a look at the ol' file!"

I had a file?

"Let's see. William Blumberg. Bill? Billy? Willy?"

"Billy," I said.

He paged through the folder, my file. My record follows me, I realized with horror, from Silver Spring to Rockville. I could go to Cleveland or California or China and my file would follow me. I could go to the moon, and that manila folder would be there, floating beside me in zero gravity.

"Let's see what we've got here, Billy. Workin' hard or hardly workin'?"

"Working hard."

"I can see that—A's as far as the eye can see. Super!"

I wished I could take a peek at those pages. Did they hold other things besides grades?

"Hmm," he said with a weird smile. His eyebrows arched a little. "A 'C' in sixth-grade science. Oops! What happened?"

"There was this science fair."

"Uh, huh," he said, still reading. His eyes widened and the fake smile disappeared. Now he didn't look jolly at all. "Hmm," he said, focusing on something else in my file. He took another sip of coffee. "Hmm. So how are you holding up, Billy?"

"Okay."

"So you move to Rockville in the middle of the school year, you're in a strange school, don't know a living soul. Must be tough for you? Is it?"

"I guess."

"Do you, uh, want to talk about it?"

"Talk about what?"

Mr. Wilson took another gulp from his coffee mug. His face lit up, the smile back, faker than before. "Do you know what they say about school guidance counselors?"

"No."

"Well, those who can't do, teach, and those who can't teach become guidance counselors." He put down his coffee and laughed. Ho, ho, ho.

"You can tell me anything, Billy," he said. "Do you know what confidentiality means?"

"It means you can't tell anybody whatever I tell you. I think it's against the law or something."

"Ah yes. The law." He leaned back in his chair. "Before I became an educator, I spent a year in law school. Studying the law is about one question and one question only: *What is the law?* That's it. That's what it all boils down to. *What is the law.*"

What was he talking about? Wasn't the law written down in some law book or in the Constitution? If you wanted to know *what is the law*, why not just look it up, like you look up a word in a dictionary? I could still hear the mimeograph machine. Clack, clack, clack. I decided that a mimeograph machine clacking was the fourth loneliest sound in the world, behind the sound of a distant lawn mower, the scratching of leaves being raked, and the sound of uproarious laughter from far away. Mr. Wilson was almost done talking about "the law." How much longer would I have to sit here?

"So, Billy, how are you, uh, coping? What's going on in your head right now?"

"Nothing."

"Come on. There's got to be something crackling in those synapses!"

He smiled at me and sipped his coffee. Oh God, it's morning. If he loved Virginia so much, why was he working at a school in Maryland? Why wasn't there a law about that? I looked out the window onto the parking lot and saw two school buses side by side, facing opposite directions. The drivers were talking and gesturing through open windows. It had started to rain. They closed their windows and the buses slowly pulled apart.

"Do you have any problems or questions you want to ask me?" Mr. Wilson put down his empty coffee cup.

"Well," I said. "I sort of can't figure out how to open my locker."

He stood up and motioned me to do the same. "I think you'll find that West Montgomery is the school with a heart," he said. "As long as you follow the rules and work hard, you're going to be very happy here. It's going to be tough at first, being the new kid, but things are going to get better real soon. I promise."

THAT NIGHT my mother came home at 5:30 from her job in Potomac. The first thing she said to me was not "Hi, Billy" or "How was your first day." It was: "I got a call at work from some idiot counselor at your school." She looked at me like it was my fault.

"Mr. Wilson? He called you?" So much for confidentiality and the Constitution. "What did he say?"

"He said you're depressed and they're going to keep an eye on you." She poked a package of ground meat that had been thawing all day.

"He really said that?" I asked. "What else did he say?"

"He said you seemed morose."

"What's morose?"

"Moping around. Feeling sorry for yourself." She threw her keys onto the counter.

"I was nervous," I said. "It was my first day."

"I know it's not easy," my mother said. She looked tired and tried to smile. "But it will get better. I promise."

"Has your new job gotten better?" I asked. She complained about it all the time.

"That's different," she said. "We're talking about you and your new school."

"How is it different?"

"You've only been there one day. Why don't you give it a chance?"

"Because I don't want to."

"Wonderful!" she exploded. She exploded a lot lately. "As if I don't already have enough to worry about. Look. Your father left us nothing. We had to move. You have to start at a new school. That's just the way it is. Why do you have to tell our problems to some stranger?"

"I didn't say anything!"

"Billy," she said, "just tell these people what they want to hear."

"What do you think I did?" I ran off to my little room with the bare walls in our crappy apartment off Rockville Pike. I flopped down on my bed. Mr. Wilson told my mother I was "morose," but didn't I say "Good morning, God" just like he wanted? What else was I supposed to say? Had he written the word "morose" in my file, and would it follow me forever? And now my mother told me that my father had left us "nothing," and did that mean this was all his fault? And if it was all his fault, wasn't it all my fault too?

A COUPLE OF WEEKS PASSED. I was following the rules and working hard and nothing was getting better. I had no friends. I decided that—aside from my mother—I would never see a familiar face again. I would be surrounded by strangers, forever lost, wandering through confusing West Montgomery hallways, stumbling across unfamiliar Rockville streets.

I settled into a routine. After school I had two hours until my mother came home from work. There wasn't anything to do. I would stop at the 7-Eleven on my way home from school. I would walk past the counter, not making eye contact with the bald guy who ran the place. I would head straight for the candy rack and check whether they had my all-time favorite candy—Good 'n Fruity.

They didn't. But there was always an empty space next to the boxes of Good 'n Plenty. Wasn't it logical to assume that the space next to the Good 'n Plenties was kept vacant, because the 7-Eleven was awaiting the Good 'n Fruity delivery, which could arrive at any day and any time, between 7:00 a.m. and 11:00 p.m.? My old 7-Eleven in Silver Spring always had Good 'n Fruity in stock, just like this Rockville 7-Eleven always had plenty of Good 'n Plenties, which were just black licorice with a black or white candy coating. The coating was okay, but the chewy center tasted bitter, like medicine. How was that candy? I didn't understand.

DURING MY SECOND WEEK at West Montgomery, my social studies class began a project on "The Nations of the European Common Market." Our teacher, Mr. Pappas, explained that this was going to be a team project.

"Every member of the team takes responsibility," he told us. He was a big guy with short curly hair who liked to yell a lot. He would say something and pause, to give the awfulness time to sink in. "You will share the credit. You will share the blame. One team, one grade. You have fifteen minutes to pick a team leader and make your work assignments. Go!"

"It would behoove you," thundered Mr. Pappas as we dragged our chairs into little circles, "to use your time wisely."

Team Belgium was me, Kurt Johnson, Bob King, Julie Baines, and Stephen Danielson. They stared at me.

"You're that new kid," Johnson said. He reeked of cigarette smoke and he had whiskers growing out of his chin.

"Right," I said.

"What's your name again?"

"Billy."

Danielson drew on a piece of paper with a black Flair pen. King stared into space, like he had been hypnotized. Julie Baines twirled a strand of her hair and looked bored.

"Billy what?" said Johnson.

"Billy Blumberg."

"Where did you come from?"

"Silver Spring."

"Silver Spring! Fancy!" He shook his head, like being from Silver Spring was something any normal person would be embarrassed about.

"You Jewish?" he asked.

"Yeah," I said, shrugging like it was no big deal.

"Let me ask you something. There's this thing Jews talk about all the time. Green cheese and locks."

"Green cheese and locks?" What was he talking about?

"Yeah. What is that?"

"Lox and cream cheese?" I said. "L-o-x?"

"What?"

"It's like—fish and cheese."

"No shit? Why is it called lox?"

I looked around the room. Team France was writing things down on pads of paper. Team West Germany was having a big discussion. I heard someone say the words *Volkswagen* and *sauerkraut*. One team, one grade.

"Um," I said to my team. "So, I guess we're supposed to pick a team leader?"

"I vote for you," said Johnson.

"Me too," said Julie Baines.

"Me three," said King, who had roused himself when Johnson asked if I was Jewish. Danielson kept drawing.

"Well, okay," I said, looking at my watch. Seven minutes were left before we had to break back out of our groups. In one week's time we had to present a written and oral report. I made the assignments: Johnson, geography; King, economy; Baines, government; Danielson, history. They would write a page each and I would put it all together.

"Is that okay?" I asked.

"You're the boss," said Johnson.

"Tell me again. What am I supposed to do?" Julie Baines asked.

"Okay, people! Back to your desks!" Mr. Pappas said. We dragged our chairs back to our desks. Danielson showed us the picture he had drawn. It was a naked woman with enormous breasts lying on a bed. "All right!" said Johnson. King nodded his approval. Julie Baines rolled her eyes and walked away. Johnson took the picture from Danielson and held it in front of my face.

"You like that, Blumberg?"

"Yeah," I said, shrugging, like it was no big deal.

IT WAS THURSDAY AFTERNOON, a few days later. I was watching the clock in sixth-period math. My teacher, Mr. Schultz, had covered the clock with a sign that read, *Time passes – Will you?* From my desk, I could still see the tip of the minute hand peeking from behind the sign, sweeping past three o'clock, toward the final bell at 3:45. *Today's the day*, I told myself. I had a feeling. The Good 'n Fruity shipment would have already come in a truck. A forklift would be employed, or maybe a conveyer belt stretching from the back of the truck to the 7-Eleven loading dock. The bald guy would stack the slim rectangular boxes of Good 'n Fruity on the rack, pushing aside the Good 'n Plenties to make room. I would come in on this day, a day like any other day, and see those multicolored boxes sprouting from that previously vacant space. I would buy five boxes, twenty cents a box. I would walk home and watch *Match Game 1971* while I ate one boxful of Good 'n Fruities, alternating between flavors. There were about thirty in a box, and I would eat one per minute so it would last for the whole show. Then *Let's Make a Deal* would be on and I'd eat another boxful. Then I would throw the empty boxes down the garbage chute before my mother got home. How could life get any better than that?

The school day ended. I walked to the 7-Eleven and began crossing the parking lot. At the far edge, I saw two girls and two guys leaning against a wall and smoking cigarettes. I recognized one of the girls—it was Julie Baines, from Team Belgium. I wondered what kind of progress she was making on the Belgian government. Since I was the team leader, I supposed that I was sort of like her boss. Should I talk to her? She looked at me, smiling. I looked away and kept going. She said something to her friends and she laughed—a high-pitched giggle that started strong and faded out. As I stepped onto the sidewalk in front of the 7-Eleven, I heard her laugh again.

I entered the 7-Eleven and the bald guy made a clicking sound with his tongue. He had yelled at me the day before. "You come in . . . you don't buy!" he had said. It hurt my feelings.

I headed for the candy rack. I had a premonition. Surely, the fact that Julie Baines laughed at me and the bald guy yelled at me was a sign. The fates didn't want me to find the Good 'n Fruities, but I wouldn't give up. My reward would be there, waiting for me.

But it wasn't. Not only were there no Good 'n Fruities next to the Good 'n Plenties, but no empty space either. Instead, there was a stack of Boston Baked Beans, boxes stretching upward like a big ugly weed.

I stood in front of the candy rack. Boston Baked Beans. I had never tried them before. Why would I? Why would anyone? I realized that my life was horrible. I was in the seventh grade, almost a teenager. Shouldn't I be smoking cigarettes and hanging out with girls, rather than worrying about a box of candy?

What was wrong with me? I didn't know for sure that Julie Baines was laughing at me. Maybe one of the guys she was with had just said something funny. Maybe when you smoke cigarettes you get a nicotine fit and you laugh a lot. And then I heard a woman's voice say, "Billy?!"

I whirled around.

It was Ms. Marvin. I hadn't seen her since my mom bawled her out in our basement in Silver Spring. I hadn't expected ever to see her again. Why would I?

"What are *you* doing here?" I asked.

She rolled her eyes and chuckled, like it was a question an idiot would ask.

"Buying some milk," she said.

"*Here*?"

"Believe it or not, Billy, teachers are real people. We put on our pants one leg at a time just like everybody else." She was wearing a red dress with flowers on it.

"No," I said, "I mean . . ."

She laughed. "I was just teasing. I live a few blocks from here. So how are you, Billy?"

"Okay."

"Really?" She looked skeptical. "Really okay?"

"Yes."

"How's . . ." she paused like she was clearing her throat, "your mom?"

"Fine."

We looked at each other.

"So," she said. "What are *you* doing here?"

I didn't know what to say, so I started talking about my search for Good 'n Fruities, how Good 'n Plenties were horrible, how they might as well have candies that taste like hot peppers, and how they should just put little pieces of glass in the Nestlé Crunch bars.

"Oh, Billy!" she said, laughing. She touched me on the arm. "That's why I've always liked you. But really, why don't you just ask Omar if he can order some Good 'n Fruities?"

"Who?"

"Omar. He owns the store. Do you want me to introduce you?"

"Not really."

"Do you want me to ask him?"

"No. That's okay."

"Really, I don't mind." Before I could tell her *no absolutely not under no circumstances*, she was at the counter talking to Omar. I slinked over to the magazine rack. Did they have the new *Mad Magazine*? Yes! Back in Silver Spring I had a subscription and I would get the latest issue before it arrived in the stores. But the magazine hadn't switched my mailing address yet. What if they screwed up and I never got it? Should I buy this one? Forty cents. Cheap.

Ms. Marvin was talking to this Omar guy. She told him something and he laughed loudly. He looked at me, still laughing. I grabbed the *Mad Magazine* and started leafing through. "You Know You're Really a Bore When . . ." Pretty funny. "Answers to Children's Letters—From God." Probably stupid. A satire of *The Partridge Family* they called *The Putrid Family*. Definitely funny.

Now Omar was talking to me. "Why didn't you just ask me?" he called across the store. "I'll order the Good 'n Fruity for you, okay?"

"Uh-huh," I grunted. "Thanks."

Ms. Marvin came back. "You're all set," she said. "See how easy that is?"

"I guess." I put my hand in my pocket to make sure I had my house key.

"So, how do you like West Montgomery?" she asked.

Omar was still looking at us. His bald head reflected the fluorescent light overhead.

"How did you know I go there?" I asked.

"I heard about it."

"From who?"

"I know some people there."

"You do? Who?"

"Oh, several. I don't want to name names."

Name *names*? Did these teachers think that they were in the CIA? Every year they had countywide "teachers meetings" where they drank coffee and smoked cigarettes and swapped those manila folders that held all our secrets. Once in the sixth grade, I passed by the teachers' lounge as the door was opening. Through the open crack I could smell cigarette smoke and see teachers talking. I heard someone say *I hate that little monster*, and everybody laughed. Who was the little monster? And if they were talking about this kid—the little monster—wasn't it likely that they were capable of saying anything about anybody? What did they say about me?

She touched me again on the shoulder. "I've missed you, Billy. We all have at Forest Glen. How about if I take you for some ice cream at the Baskin-Robbins? And then I can drive you home?"

"No," I said, again fingering the key in my pocket, "that's okay."

"You're sure?"

"Yeah."

"Well," she said, "take care, Billy."

"Goodbye," I said. She started to leave, then stopped and turned back toward me. She had a weird look on her face.

"I'll bet you miss your dad a lot, don't you?"

"I guess so."

"I'm sure he misses you," she said, nodding sadly.

What did that mean? My dad was dead. How could he miss anyone?

THE NEXT DAY, Team Belgium met. The team leaders were supposed to collect everything and put it all together into a final report over the weekend. I collected Team Belgium's submissions. Johnson, Danielson, and Julie Baines had done nothing. On a piece of loose-leaf notebook paper, King had written these words: *leading exports, suger beats, milk, veel.*

"Sorry, man," said Johnson. "Things to do, people to see. You know how it is."

Yeah, I knew. I would have to do the whole thing myself. I could do that. But someone else had to do the oral presentation. That was the rule. The team leader was not allowed to do the oral report.

"You do it," said Johnson to Julie Baines. King stared into space. Danielson was busy shading nipples with a No. 2 pencil. Julie stopped twirling her hair.

"No way. You do it," she said to Johnson. They both looked at me. Johnson arched his eyebrows.

"I'll write it all out for you," I said to Julie. "All you have to do is read it out loud, okay?"

"Yeah, I guess," she said.

I spent all weekend in the Rockville Library. I read the Belgium sections in the *World Book* and the *Encyclopedia Americana*. I took notes on little blue index cards. That night at home, I wrote the report. Five pages, single spaced. I drew the cover page using a multicolored pen I had gotten in the mail from Spencer Gifts. It had twelve different colors and was shaped like a missile silo. I printed "The Nation of Belgium" in big block letters, each letter written in a different color ink. Then I drew a little candy bar in brown ink, with "Belgian Chocolate" written on it. I put the report in a three-ring binder. One of the steel rings clipped my thumb as I was snapping in the pages. It broke the skin, but there was no blood.

Next, I wrote what Julie Baines was going to say in the oral report. It was kind of cool that a girl would actually be speaking words that I wrote. The words would come from my brain and she would say them as if they were her own. I decided to give her something funny to say in the beginning. It was important to set the right tone.

Report day came. I had given Julie Baines her speech before homeroom and suggested she look it over before second period.

"I hope I can read your handwriting," she said.

"I printed it."

"Whatever." She folded the paper in half and stuffed it in her notebook.

"Go!" said Mr. Pappas, a couple of hours later. Julie Baines stood at the front of the class, her eyes fixed on the page I had written. She read in a monotone. I could barely hear her:

In terms of square miles, the nation of . . . Belgium . . . is approximately the size of Maryland. Bet you all didn't know you lived in Belgium, did you?

Nobody laughed. Pappas frowned and flexed his head to the right and to the left. I could see the muscles in his thick neck. Julie Baines continued:

The nation of Belgium got its name from its first inhabitants, the . . . Bel-gae? . . . a group of mostly Celtic tribes, and from the Roman province in northern . . . Gaul . . . known as, uh, . . . Gallia? Historically, Belgium has been a part of the, um, Low Countries, which also includes the Nether Lands and Lux-en-burg . . .

"Stop!" Pappas shouted. "Do you even understand the words that are coming out of your mouth? Did you write any of this?" She looked down, stone-faced, and gave a little shrug.

Pappas turned his fury on Team Belgium. "What did each of you contribute?" he yelled.

"Lots of stuff," Johnson said.

"The part about sugar beets," King said.

"Mr. Danielson! What did you do?" said Pappas.

Danielson looked up from his drawing.

"Nothing," he said.

"D!!!" he shouted. "Team Belgium gets a D! Next up is Team West Germany."

I felt sick. I was going to get a D and I did all the work. I stood up and raised my hand.

"What is it?" Pappas said.

I heard myself say, "I don't think it's fair that I get a D."

"One team, one grade. You should have done a better job managing your team."

"But I did all the work."

"Then you broke the rules."

"But we're turning in a good report." I picked up my report and held it out as proof. Multicolored ink. A picture of a candy bar.

"Doesn't matter. In our society, it would behoove you—and all of you—to remember that if you break the law, you must pay the consequences."

"But . . . what is the law?" I said.

"What?"

"What is the law? That's what Mr. Wilson said!"

"Who??"

"My guidance counselor."

"Oh, right." He rolled his eyes. "Well, I'm your teacher, not Wilson. And if the sign says don't walk, you don't walk because that's the law."

"But, what is the law?"

"Both you—and your team—get D's. Sit down. Now."

"But what if someone is attacking you and the sign says don't walk and you have to cross the street to get away. Is *that* against the law?"

"Do you want an F for your team?"

"Is *that* against the law??"

"Okay, fine. Your team gets an F."

"*What is the law?*" I shouted. "*What is the law?*" I looked down and saw that I was still holding the report. My hands were shaking. I flipped the report onto my desk, but it skidded off the top and flopped onto the floor, face down.

"Calm down, son," Pappas said, glancing at the clock on the wall. He looked nervous. He wasn't yelling anymore. "It's okay. It's not the end of the world."

The bell rang. I gathered up my books and tried to pretend like nothing had happened. Kids were whispering and laughing and looking at me. My mind had snapped, like Ms. Marvin had said it would. I could feel the hot tears building, but I concentrated on not crying. I knew *that* particular law, the one that says if you're a guy in junior high and you cry in class, it's all over.

Julie Baines came up to me and handed me my report, which she had picked up off the floor. She looked sorry.

"You okay?" she said. She said it like she meant it. Why couldn't she talk about Belgium like she meant it? I looked away, grunting, and walked into the hallway. Why did we have to move here? This was the second worst day of my life. My next class, third period, was PE. We were going to be tortured on the gymnasium apparatus.

"Hey, Blumberg!" I heard. I turned and Johnson was coming for me. I had just gotten him an F. Was he going to kill me now?

He grabbed me by the shoulder. But he was smiling. "Man, that was awesome—I don't know what the fuck you were talking about, but whatever it was, you kicked Pappas's ass!"

"Sorry we got an F," I said.

"Shit, man. I get F's all the time," he said. "It's not so bad."

I GOT THROUGH THE DAY. My strategy was not to look anyone in the face. Finally, I sat in my last class, math class, sixth period. *Time passes – Will you?* Fifteen minutes to go. And then I could walk to the 7-Eleven, buy a *Mad Magazine* plus a box of Good 'n Fruities, and go home and watch *Match Game 1971*.

The classroom door opened and a teacher's aide came in. She had a note.

"Blumberg!" Mr. Schultz growled, motioning toward me. *Uh-oh,* I heard someone whisper from behind me.

It was a hall pass to the Administrative Office. "Report immediately," it said. Report to who? The vice principal, the principal, the Superintendent of Montgomery County Public Schools? It didn't say.

I walked through empty shiny hallways. This was it. I was getting an F in social studies and I was about to be suspended or expelled or put in reform school for yelling *What is the law?* at a teacher. Why did they wait so long? Maybe they had a big teachers meeting to decide what to do with me. I was the little monster. If so, maybe I should start acting like one. Johnson said that getting F's wasn't so bad. Maybe he was right.

In the Administrative Office, I handed the secretary my note. She told me to "proceed" back to Mr. Wilson's office. This could be a good sign. Mr. Wilson was jolly. And I had defended his "What is the law."

His door was closed. From behind it I could hear voices, a man and a woman talking and laughing. I knocked and the voices stopped.

"Come in."

I opened the door.

"Hello, Billy," said Ms. Marvin. She was sitting in the chair facing Wilson's desk. He was leaning back, his hands clasped behind his head. His grinning face got all serious.

"Ms. Marvin and I go way back," he said. "I told her about what happened and we thought you might appreciate seeing a familiar face."

"We're all very concerned about you, Billy," she said.

Mr. Wilson looked at a big clock that hung on the wall. He stood up and took the coat draped over the back of his chair. "I leave you in her capable hands!" he said, as if delivering a line in a play. And then he left.

Ms. Marvin rolled her eyes. "How he keeps his job, I'll never know. So, what do you say, Billy? Let's get out of this hellhole."

"Are you going to tell my mother?" I said.

"Of course not."

"Mr. Wilson did."

"I'm not Mr. Wilson."

"Isn't he your friend?"

"Mr. Wilson and I are acquaintances. You and I are friends. There's a big difference."

I looked at the clock. There were seven minutes to go until the final bell. Now what?

"So let's go," she said.

"Where are we going?"

"How about that ice cream?"

"I need to get my jacket and books and stuff," I said. "It's all in my locker."

Five minutes to go. We headed to my locker. "Ah yes, junior high," she said. "It's pure hell, isn't it? Little innocent children come in here like freshly minted pennies, bright and shiny. They get circulated, rolled and stomped on, nicked, scratched up, and encrusted with filth. By the time they get to high school you can't tell whether the face on that penny is Abraham Lincoln or Donald Duck. And take it from me, by the time you get to be my age, the face on that penny is grotesque beyond description. Your dad was a principal, so he knew, didn't he?"

I didn't have time for this. The bell was about to ring and everyone would see me with Ms. Marvin. We got to my locker. I was getting pretty good with the combination lock, but my hands were shaking and I couldn't get it to open. 25-10-37. 25-10-37. "Relax," Ms. Marvin said, "take your time."

Easy for her to say. 25-10-37. 25-10-37. The lock clicked open and I jerked back the locker door. A piece of notebook paper fluttered out and fell at our feet. It was Danielson's picture—the woman with the big breasts lying on a bed.

"What have we here?" Ms. Marvin said, picking it up.

"It's not mine!"
"Of course not."
The final bell rang.

. 4 .

Metal Is Metal

THE MERV GRIFFIN SHOW, Wednesday evening, the living room sofa: me, my mother, my father. It was late August, between sixth and seventh grade. Merv Griffin's guest was the Israeli psychic, Uri Geller, who could bend spoons and guess the contents of closed envelopes. Merv Griffin asked Uri Geller why he couldn't bend the metal in Arab tanks during the Six Day War. Geller said that he tried really hard and that he would have if he could have. Then they broke for a commercial.

"How do the 'spirits' know if the metal is in a tank or in a spoon?" said my mother.

My father chuckled. "You don't understand."

"What's not to understand? Metal is metal."

I watched an Anacin commercial where people who suffered horrible headaches were now smiling and enjoying themselves.

"You can't apply scientific principles to the spiritual world. Who knows what physical laws apply?" my father said. "Who can say?"

"I can say. It's a bunch of baloney. Who has time for such nonsense?"

"Maybe I do."

"Since when are you such a big expert on this mishegas?"

"Since I opened my eyes. Since I opened my mind," he said, pausing. "Since I opened my heart. Maybe you should try it sometime."

My mother stood up.

"Just spare me," she said. "And tell me this, if you know so much. Why would God the almighty, God of Abraham, God of Isaac, God of Jacob keep that little putz Uri Geller from disabling a tank bent on destroying the Jewish people, while at the same time allowing him to bend a tablespoon on the Merv Griffin show? Why would He in His infinite wisdom do that? *Why?*" She stormed out of the room.

My father shrugged. "Who are we to question?" He flashed his sheepish grin. "Am I right?"

"Guess so," I said. The bedroom door slammed. The Anacin commercial was over.

"SO . . . WHAT TIME does your mom get home from work?" Ms. Marvin asked. We were driving in her yellow VW Bug. She was taking me to her apartment.

"5:30."

"Don't worry," she said. "You'll be home in plenty of time."

I took a bite out of my ice cream cone, three scoops of pink bubblegum flavor from Baskin-Robbins. After buying me the ice cream, she said she wanted to invite me to her apartment because she had something to show me that would "expand my consciousness." I said no that's okay and thanks for the ice cream. She asked me what I would be doing if I was at home. I said I would be watching *Match Game 1971*.

"Listen to me, Billy," she said, as I balanced my triple dipper outside the Baskin-Robbins. "Thirty years from now will be the year 2001. You may be dead by then, if not sooner. But if you are alive in 2001, I *guarantee* you will not remember a single episode of *Match Game 1971*."

"Okay."

"But you will remember what I plan on showing you in my apartment today. I promise."

"Well. Okay." In thirty years, I would be a grown-up and I'd come home from some horrible job and watch *Match Game 2001*. Ms. Marvin was right. How would I possibly remember anything about *Match Game 1971*, much less 1981 or 1991? I had nothing to look forward to.

We drove past softball fields. I finished eating the ice cream cone and started chewing the wad of bubble gum that had grown in my mouth. Ms. Marvin kept looking at me while she drove. I watched the road. What was she going to show me in her apartment? Maybe it was the knife or the candlestick she would use to finish me off. In the sixth grade, Ms. Marvin read us an Edgar Allan Poe story every Friday afternoon. "The Pit and the Pendulum." "The Tell-Tale Heart." "The Masque of the Red Death." Raising her eyebrows she would grin, and snapping the book shut, say *the end, or is it?* Then she would tell us to have a nice weekend.

We stopped at a red light. Now she was talking about Mr. Wilson, what a terrible guidance counselor he was and how he didn't care about kids and only cared about teacher pensions and summer vacations. Mr. Wilson's name was Burt.

Maybe she wouldn't murder me because, except for the guy at Baskin-Robbins, Mr. Wilson would be the last person to see me alive. Cooperating with the cops when a seventh-grader in your school gets butchered is definitely "the law." On the other hand, what if Mr. Wilson was an accomplice? I decided that if

Mr. Wilson was waiting for us in her apartment and drinking coffee out of his *Virginia is for Lovers* mug, I would make a run for it. Maybe I could climb out the window. What floor did she live on?

She looked over at me, one eyebrow raised. "Burt and I, we go way back. He's always had a thing for me. But I mean, please. He wouldn't even know where to put it."

The light turned green. She was still looking at me, with this weird smile, as if we both knew something that nobody else knew. "Uh, green," I said. "The light's green."

"I'm not supposed to talk like that in front of my students," she said. "Only you're not my student anymore, are you?"

"I guess not, Ms. Marvin."

"My first name is Nancy. Call me Nancy."

"Okay."

"So say, 'Hey there, Nancy.' Say it."

"Hey there, Nancy," I said.

The car behind us honked.

She stomped on the gas pedal and we lurched forward. We passed the Rockville municipal swimming center. I had learned how to swim there last summer, at day camp. On Tuesdays and Thursdays, we took a bus from Silver Spring to Rockville. I had bad ears but I decided not to worry about it. I dove and swam and had a great time. By the end of the summer I had two thunderous, pulsing earaches. *I told you not to get in the water*, my mom said. She had to take me to the doctor. My dad said, *Well, you had fun and you learned how to swim. What's a little pain?* The doctor stuck a big syringe into my ear and punctured my eardrum. It was the worst pain I ever felt.

Now Ms. Marvin had gotten quiet, like she was concentrating on her driving. Mr. Wilson didn't know where to put it. Put what where? There was a game show on TV called *The Who, What, or Where Game*. Maybe that was the show I would remember in thirty years.

MY FATHER AND I finished watching *The Merv Griffin Show*. Uri Geller bent some spoons and guessed some drawings. A pyramid, a flower, and a barn. My father turned off the TV.

"So, tell me," he said, in a lowered voice, "what do you think of all this?"

I heard the bedroom door open. My mother stomped into the kitchen.

"All this what?" I asked.

"This Uri Geller business," he said, pointing to the shiny gray TV screen. I could see our reflections—ghosts sitting on a sofa.

"When people talk about the spirit world and ESP and all that stuff," I asked, "they're talking about God, right?"

"Probably."

"Then . . . why *would* God let Uri Geller bend tablespoons but not tanks?" I watched my ghost push its glasses up the bridge of its nose.

My father nodded vigorously, as if he'd been waiting for just that particular question.

"Okay, let me put it this way." He grabbed a copy of *Commentary* magazine that was sitting on the coffee table. The cover said, REVOLUTIONISM AND THE JEWS. "Is a hamster capable of understanding the concepts in this magazine?"

"No," I said. "Neither am I." *Commentary* was the most boring magazine in the world. There were no pictures and no ads, just fat solid paragraphs that never ended. It was worse than reading the phone book.

"Okay, okay. What I'm trying to say is that there's a whole spiritual world swirling around each of us. If you can't see it or touch it, how can you possibly understand it?"

"What does that have to do with Uri Geller?"

I could hear the sound of banging drawers and clanging pans. He shifted on his sofa cushion.

"Think of it this way. You go to school, right?"

"Right."

"You talk to your friends. You sit in class. You listen to your teachers. That's your world."

"I guess so."

"But there's a whole other parallel world you don't see. There are the parents and the teachers and the principal and all these people have conversations and hold meetings and discuss issues that affect you."

"Are you talking about how teachers sit in the teachers' lounge and talk about the students behind their backs?"

"Sort of." He stopped and thought for a moment. "What if," he said, "you could hear what they're saying in the teachers' lounge?"

"I'd know who was about to get in trouble. I'd know all the other kids' secrets."

"Yes. And let's say you had the power to peer into the teachers' lounge whenever you wanted. What do you think that would be like? How do you think it would feel?"

"Pretty cool."

My mother started crying in the kitchen. My father sighed.

"Is Mom okay?" I said.

WE DROVE into downtown Rockville and turned left into a towering apartment building complex. We rolled down a steep driveway that ended in front of a scratched-up garage door. Ms. Marvin lowered her window and stuck a plastic card into a box. The garage door opened slowly, squeakily. She looked at me, smiling.

"Open sesame," she said.

My peppermint bubble gum had lost its flavor. My jaws were tired.

"Do you and your mom have a cool garage like this?" she asked, pulling into a parking spot.

"Not really. It's just a boring parking lot."

She shut off the engine and opened her door. "Time to enter the forbidden temple," she said. "We're going to need that box on the back seat. Could you grab it for me, Billy?"

It was a jigsaw puzzle box with a rubber band around it. On the box was a picture of the Eiffel Tower. This was going to expand my consciousness? The thing about jigsaw puzzles is, you take an hour to put together two or three pieces, then you give up. I grabbed the box off the back seat.

It definitely was not a box of puzzle pieces. Things rolled and rattled inside, pieces of something heavy. Bone fragments? Eyeballs? Shrunken heads? I imagined myself slowly opening the box and screaming in horror.

"What time is it now?" she asked as we waited for an elevator.

I pressed the button on my digital watch. "4:15," I said.

We got on the elevator. She pushed the "7" button.

Then she said: "When you die, what do you think happens to you?"

"Um, I don't know."

"Haven't you ever thought about it?"

"Not really." The elevator bell dinged. One . . . two . . . three.

"Well, think about it now. What do you think happens?"

"Probably nothing."

"Why do you say that? What's your evidence?"

"Um," I said. "There were all those years before I was born. Nothing was happening to me then."

"Really. I wouldn't be too sure about that." Five . . . six . . . seven.

The elevator door opened. I twisted the rubber band on the Eiffel Tower box.

"I'm going to tell you something about myself," she said.

"Okay."

"I don't tell very many people this."

"Okay." I followed her out of the elevator.

"This isn't a joke," she said over her shoulder as I trailed her down the dimly lit hallway. "Do you understand?"

"Yes."

She stopped in front of apartment 714. "I believe in past lives—do you know what that means?" she said.

"Not really."

"It means that your spirit has lived before you. For example, I know that one of my past lives was as a nobleman in eighteenth-century France. He was executed during the French Revolution. Decapitation. His head in a basket."

"How do you know?"

"Because sometimes I wake up in the morning with a sharp pain in the back of my neck. I can almost feel the guillotine blade slicing clean through."

She put the key in the lock, then turned to me. "Have you ever felt that way?"

"Uh . . . sometimes I wake up in the middle of the night

with a stomachache," I said. "Does that mean one of my past-life guys got—like—stabbed in the stomach?"

She opened the door. "Could be."

The living room was shady and humid. There were plants everywhere—hanging from the ceiling, spilling over on the bookshelves. Weird paintings and drawings hung on the walls, lines and arrows that twisted and doubled back and branched off like maps to nowhere. On a mantel ledge separating the living room from the dining room was a row of bug-eyed wooden dolls, their mouths in horrified "O" shapes. The dining room table was round with a dark red tablecloth. Four chairs. No sign of Mr. Wilson drinking coffee.

Ms. Marvin closed the front door behind us. "Home sweet home," she said.

"A lot of the time in the spring?" I offered, "I wake up all stuffed up because I have hay fever. What does that mean?"

"Who knows?" she said. "Maybe you died of pneumonia or tuberculosis. We can find out. Not today, though." She took off her jacket.

A dark brown cat came straight for me. I tried to deflect it with my shoe.

"Don't be afraid. She likes you."

It was trying to rub up against my ankle.

"Her name is The Black Cat, after the Edgar Allan Poe story."

"But it's brown," I said.

"It's called *irony*. When you grow up, you'll understand."

I sneezed. "I'm allergic to cats, too."

She scooped up the cat in her arms and held it close to her face. She turned to me and pointed The Black Cat's head in my direction.

"Your dad believed in past lives," said Ms. Marvin. "Did he ever talk to you about that?"

MY FATHER SAID, "Your mother is fine."

"Then why is she crying?"

"When your mother says things like 'metal is metal' and ridicules that which she doesn't understand, it's very unfortunate. She's missing out because there's a whole other world she doesn't understand."

"The world of Uri Geller?"

"Forget Uri Geller. I'm talking about something much more important." He leaned close. He lowered his voice to a whisper.

"Do you remember how I was in a bad way last spring and earlier this summer? How I was sad all the time? How I didn't want to go to work anymore?"

"Yes."

"Your mother and the rabbi and Feinbaum wanted me to fool around with some psychiatrist. I didn't go. Do you remember that?"

"Yes."

"Well, a wonderful thing has happened to me this summer, and now I'm happier than I've ever been. And guess what? I'm ready to go back to work. Do you know why?"

"No."

"I decided to place my faith in forces greater than science."

"What does that mean?" I said.

"Murray, would you come in here?" my mother said, from the bedroom. "Now."

My father exhaled slowly. "Ah yes. Here we go."

"WHAT TIME is it now?"

I pressed the button on my digital watch. "4:34." Ms. Marvin and I were sitting across from each other at the round table with the red tablecloth. Between us sat the Eiffel Tower puzzle box. Around the room, she had lit long sticks that glowed at the end, spewing out wisps of smoke. It made the place smell like a urinal cake.

"How would you like to cast some spells, Billy?" she said.

"Sure . . ."

She pulled the rubber band off the puzzle box and opened it. Inside were five thick black candles. She placed one in the center of the table.

"Here's how it works. There are good spells and bad spells."

"Okay."

"You give me a list of people. And then things happen to them."

"Okay."

She struck a match and lit the black candle.

"Which kind of spells do you want to do?" she asked. "The good ones or the hexes?"

"Which ones do you want me to do?"

She smiled. "Up to you. Hexes are good for revenge."

"Can I put myself on the good spell list?"

"No," she said, kind of annoyed. "It doesn't work that way."

"Then I choose . . . hexes," I said. A bead of black wax slowly dripped down the side of the candle.

"Okay," she said, adjusting the candle so that it was in the very center of the table. "This is very serious business. A hex on someone could result in anything bad—from dying a horrible death to something like getting locked out of their house or losing their wallet. Are you sure you want to proceed?"

"I'm sure."

She stared at me, her eyes narrowing. "One more thing before we start. This is very important. If you tell anybody about this, the hex will turn on your head and you will be cursed. Do you understand?"

"Yes."

"Say: I understand."

"I understand."

"Okay. Good. Give me the first name."

"Bob Short," I said.

"Who's that?"

"He owns the Senators. He's moving them to Texas."

"All right," she said, writing the name down on a piece of notebook paper. "Who else?"

"Brooks Robinson."

"Who?"

"He's on the Orioles. I hate him."

She sighed and wrote down Brooks Robinson's name. "Look," she said, "this will work best with people you know personally." And why is that, I wondered. Metal is metal. Why couldn't it work on anybody, whether it was someone famous or some guy down the street? Was there a rule written down somewhere? What was the law?

"So who else?" she asked. "Who did something bad to you or to someone you love? Who needs to pay for it?"

I thought for a few seconds. "Michael Strohman."

She looked at me.

"Just some kid at Sligo." She wrote down *Michael Strohman*. "Who else?"

"Mr. Pappas. He's my social studies teacher and he gave me a D I didn't even deserve and when I complained he gave me an F."

"Done. Next."

"Kurt Johnson, Bob King, Julie Baines, and Stephen Danielson." Team Belgium. She wrote down all the names, the pencil squeaking.

"Who else?" she said.

It was like when I used to go with my father to the deli on Sunday afternoons. He would order one thing at a time—a quarter pound of corned beef, a pickled tomato—and the guy behind the counter would say "What else?" This would repeat again and again, practically forever, until my father would answer, *What else? Nothing else.*

"Actually," I said, "take Julie Baines off the list."

"Wonderful," Ms. Marvin said, putting a line through *Julie Baines*. "Now we're going in the wrong direction. How about Harold Feinbaum?"

My father's old boss, the president of Beth Israel Congregation.

"How do you know about him?" I asked.

"I know about a lot of things," she said, with a smile. She added *Harold Feinbaum* to the list. Then she scraped some black wax with her finger and made it into a little ball.

"You know what?" Ms. Marvin said, pulling the list toward her and grabbing the pencil again. "Either this list doesn't have enough names, or . . . it doesn't have the *right* names. How about . . ." she said, "we put Harold's son on the list too?"

"Lawrence?! You know him?"

"The boy who threw the paper airplane. Right?"

What else did she know? That if Young Mr. Katz hadn't lost control of the class, and if Lawrence Feinbaum hadn't thrown the paper airplane, my father wouldn't have come in and he wouldn't have been smacked in the head with the paper airplane and his yarmulke wouldn't have popped off and I wouldn't have laughed at him and he wouldn't have gotten all depressed again and killed himself? He put his faith in forces greater than science. And it worked! But then I undid all of it. Maybe I should put myself on the list?

She put the ball of wax on top of the piece of paper with the names of the doomed on it. "Now," she said, taking a deep breath, "there's one more thing we must do. Are you sure you want to proceed?"

"I guess so."

"Once this is done, it's done and nearly impossible to take back. Do you understand?"

"So what happens to the people on the list?"

"I told you. Something a little bit bad or something really bad."

"When will it happen?"

"It's impossible to know exactly."

She put down her pencil and looked at me, her face serious.

"We need to summon your father. He can intercede on your behalf in order to enact the hexes."

"What are you talking about?" I said. "He's dead."

She shook her head. "Remember when I said our spirits inhabit past lives? Well, they continue to live beyond our current lives too."

"So . . ." I started slowly, "is he in somebody else's body now? Like your ghost was in the French guy?"

"Probably. The important thing is he's still very present. He's not gone."

"But if his spirit is in some other person, it would have to be in a little baby? Like in someplace like France?"

"Perhaps."

"So if we summoned him, would the French baby have to be here, or would the spirit leave the baby?"

"Well—obviously—the baby wouldn't have to be here."

"But what would happen to that baby while the spirit is flying from France to Rockville? Wouldn't the baby die? Would my father's spirit have to find another baby being born somewhere in the world? What if we summon him and he's got no place to go back to?"

Ms. Marvin rolled the black ball of wax off the list of names. "Would you like me to take you home, Billy?"

"Yes," I said. "I mean, no." Metal was probably metal. But what if it wasn't?

"Fine." She rolled the ball back onto the list. "Now. I have to ask you this question. Do you want me to summon your father's spirit to help us enact the hexes?"

"Okay."

"I need you to tell me how your father died."

"Why do you need to know that?"

"I don't want to go into a bunch of technical explanations. Just tell me."

"Well . . . he committed suicide."

"*How* did he do it?"

"I don't know."

"What do you mean you don't know?"

"My mom never told me."

"You're kidding!" she said. "That figures."

"So . . . I guess we can't do this?" I asked. Now I really did want to go home.

"Of course we can. Since you're his flesh and blood that will be sufficient to summon his spirit."

I looked at the top of the Eiffel Tower puzzle box, still on the table. The puzzle pieces must have been discarded somewhere—at the bottom of a sock drawer, in the trunk of a car, deep in a bag of trash at the bottom of a landfill. It would take days to retrieve them, even more days to put them all together.

"So what do we do now?" I said. "Some sort of ceremony?"

"Some sort of ceremony!" She got mad. "Do you think this is a joke? Do you think I'm going to chant some gibberish and smear chicken blood on my face?"

"No."

"This is the real thing. You just think it and it happens." The candle was burning, the wax dripping.

"Can you feel his presence?" she whispered. "Your hex list is being enacted on the spiritual plane." I smelled peppermint on her breath.

I could feel that brown cat rubbing up against my leg. My father hated cats, didn't he? Once he came home from work with a story about one of the teachers at his school whose cat had scratched up the living room sofa. *Get rid of it!* my father said, shaking his head in amazement as he told us the story. *Who needs it?* my mother said, laughing and nodding. They agreed. They both hated cats. My father and my mother both hated cats and they loved each other and they loved me. What other conclusion was possible?

I decided that if my father's spirit was really in the room, the cat would drop dead or at the very least be shooed away by a ghostly hand.

The cat kept rubbing up against my leg.

"Do you feel his presence?" she repeated, louder.

"I don't feel anything," I said. "My father is dead."

"Fine," she said. She blew out the candle. Then she buried her face in her hands. "Oh, Murray," she said. "I tried." She stood up and, without even looking at me, walked out of the room. I heard her bedroom door close.

I sat there, watching the smoke curling out of the black candle.

Murray. That was my father's first name. When they met each other at that parent-teacher conference, did she say *Nice to meet you, Mr. Blumberg*, and did he say *Call me Murray*? She had told me to call her Nancy. *Say it*, she had said.

Again, the cat rubbed against my leg. Did my father sit here during the summer, at this round red table, in this metal folding chair, staring at that candle and the Eiffel Tower box? The Black Cat. What kind of name was that? *It's called irony*, she had said. What if you had this cat and you introduced him to someone. You'd say: "Hello, I'd like you to meet my brown cat, The Black Cat." Was that irony? And when my father was sitting here feeling The Black Cat rub against his leg, did he say, "Oh, what a cute little kitty?" Was that irony, too?

I pushed the cat away with my foot. From her bedroom, I heard a sharp gurgling sound, like something between a gasp and a sob. I pushed the button on my digital watch. 5:15. My mother would be home in fifteen minutes.

I went over to her bedroom door. I stood there, breathing. Maybe she would sense I was waiting and come out. I could hear a faint whimper and some whispering. Who was she talking to? 5:17. 5:18. I knocked softly.

"Ms. Marvin?" No response. "Um, Nancy?"

"Go back to the table. I'll be out in a minute." Her voice was sharp and mean.

"I, uh, need to go home. My mom is coming home from work at 5:30."

"Oh, God. Don't worry about it."

I heard The Black Cat meow. It was staring at me. *Get out,* it seemed to be saying, *while you still can.* I walked over to the round table and picked up the list of hex victims—*Harold Feinbaum, Lawrence Feinbaum, etc., etc.* I put the hex list in my pocket.

"Billy?" I heard Ms. Marvin say from her bedroom. Now she sounded sad. "I'm sorry. Everything's going to be all right, honey."

Where did I belong? Not in my sixth-grade teacher's apartment, smelling of cat and urinal cakes, somewhere in Rockville. Not with my sixth-grade teacher, who *ordered* me to call her Nancy. She called me "honey." How big could Rockville be? I would find my own way home. I went quickly through the living room, trying not to look at her bedroom door, walking not running to the nearest exit. The apartment door slammed behind me as I ran down the hallway. I pressed the down button and the elevator door opened, as if it had been waiting there just for me.

. 5 .
Official Worries

I WANDERED THE STREETS OF ROCKVILLE, shuffling over narrow sidewalks next to a torrent of swirling traffic and honking horns. I imagined one of the cars jumping the curb and plowing into me. Ms. Marvin asked me what it would be like to be dead. First, I'd get hit by the car and tossed into the air like a hand puppet, limbs flailing, head bobbing. Then I'd land and a steamroller would mash me flat like pizza dough. The police would come and stretch yellow crime-scene tape around the perimeter of my broken body. My crushed personal effects would be catalogued: plastic owl-shaped eyeglasses with thick lenses and brown frames, Pre-Algebra book, loose-leaf notebook, house key. *What have we here?* one of the cops would say, holding a piece of lined notebook paper up to the streetlight. A list with mysterious names, written in mysterious handwriting! *Harold Feinbaum, Lawrence Feinbaum, Michael Strohman.* Suspects? Or victims?

Downtown Rockville was a confusing jumble of pavement in the shadow of Rockville Mall, a massive windowless monstrosity that seemed to swallow up several blocks. I was lost. I passed by a gas station and a Suburban Trust bank. The sign flashed: 5:30 PM, 51 F. My mom would be walking through the door. She would be frowning and shaking her head because no strains of *Match Game 1971* would be spilling out from my bedroom. I hoped she wouldn't call the police. How embarrassing would it be for a squad car to come screeching over, sirens blaring, to gather up a twelve-year-old kid who was lost?

I saw a man coming out of the bank. He was wearing a suit and tie and he carried a briefcase. "Excuse me, sir?" I said. I hated talking to strangers. My voice squeaked and it was like I was five years old.

"Are you lost, son?" he asked.

"Sort of."

He gave me directions. After ten minutes, I reached the shopping center with the 7-Eleven and the Baskin-Robbins. It was 5:42 and what difference would five minutes make? I went into the 7-Eleven. That Omar guy wasn't behind the counter, just some high school kid. Good sign. I hurried over to the candy aisle. The boxes of Boston Baked Beans were gone. Another good sign. And then—at long last—the Good 'n Fruities were there for the taking. My heart did not burst with joy, like I had expected. It was just okay. I bought a box and stuffed it into my pocket. 5:48.

I crossed the parking lot and headed toward my apartment building.

Ms. Marvin. She was crazy, wasn't she? Her mind had snapped and it stayed snapped, just like they always say you can't unscramble an egg or put toothpaste back in a tube. I hated her in the sixth grade when she gave me a C-minus on my science project. Then I liked her that one time in the 7-Eleven. But now, I guessed I hated her again. On the other hand, my dad liked her. And I liked my dad. So did that mean I was supposed to like Ms. Marvin? Is that how it worked? On the other hand, if I hated Ms. Marvin and my mom hated her, did that mean that maybe my mom wasn't so bad?

I reached my building. Going into the lobby, I pretended that I was living in our house in Silver Spring, that my father was alive, that suddenly I had leapt forward in time and here I was walking into a strange and ugly apartment building in some crappy city with a ridiculous name like "Rockville." What was I doing here? Maybe I was a secret agent gathering intelligence. But for what and for whom I couldn't imagine. I got on the elevator and pushed the "5" button. There was a sign on the door warning tenants not to throw objects out of their windows. What kind of person would throw an object out of a window, and what kind of building would allow that kind of person to live here?

I got off the elevator and walked down a long hallway with greenish brownish grayish carpeting. I smelled whiffs of people's dinners and heard snippets of conversations, short bursts of television laughter. I stopped in front of apartment 5E. Look—there was a key in my pocket! I put it in the lock and twisted, clockwise. Open sesame.

"Where were you?" my mother said. She was standing in the middle of the living room, her eyes on me like some raygun that could blast deep into my bones.

"Answer me!"

Why did she have to shout? I could hear the man next door when he shouted. He was a pudgy guy who looked like Tim Conway from *McHale's Navy*. Sometimes late at night, I would hear him yelling at somebody from the other side of my bedroom wall. He would shout, "What I'm saying is . . . ," but I could never quite get what he was saying.

"Do you have any idea how worried sick I was?" my mother

said. "For all I knew, you could have been lying in a ditch somewhere!"

"Sorry," I said, fingering the box of Good 'n Fruities in my pocket. So let's say I was hit by a car and thrown in the air and landed—*in a ditch*—and then was crushed flat by the steamroller. What if the box of Good 'n Fruities they found in my pocket was perfect and crisp, like it just came from the factory? That would be another mystery.

"What is that in your pocket?" she said.

I pulled out the Good 'n Fruities, leaving the list of names in my pocket.

"Don't eat junk before dinner," she said, a bit calmer. "Now where were you?"

I told her I was with a friend of mine from school.

"What's his name?" she said.

"Kurt Johnson," I said. I couldn't think of anyone else.

"Who's that?"

"Just some kid in school."

"Dear God, I need this like a hole in the head. Can you be more specific?" We were still standing in the middle of the living room.

"Well," I stammered, "he's this kid in my social studies class and we were working in the Rockville Library concerning our social studies project concerning the nation of Belgium."

"I thought you were finished with that."

"Yes, but we're supposed to do more for extra credit."

She looked me up and down, like she was inspecting the boys' suits hanging from a rack at Sears.

"Why are you so late? Didn't you know what time it was?"

"We were working so hard we didn't notice."

"And this boy was with you the whole time?"

"Yes."

"Okay. So where is it? Let me see it."

"Where is what?"

"What do you think—the extra credit! All that work you did after school."

"Kurt's got it," I said.

"Naturally. So tell me, just exactly who is this Kurt character?"

"I told you! Just some kid from school."

"What does his father do?"

"How should I know?"

"You could ask."

"What if he asks what *my* father does?"

She turned away and retreated to the kitchen. I took off my jacket. I heard pots clanking together. "Dinner in twenty minutes," she shouted. "Wash your hands."

Dinner was macaroni and cheese. We sat across from each other, as if we were each eating in a room alone, spearing our respective portions of macaroni and cheese with our respective forks. My mother shook her head and muttered *help me something something*—I couldn't make out what she was saying. Who was she talking to? My father? Was her mind snapping too?

I nudged my pants pocket and felt the outlines of the folded-up piece of paper, that list of names in Ms. Marvin's handwriting. I concentrated on my macaroni and cheese. If you attached all the pieces of macaroni end-to-end, you would have a long squiggly tube. I read somewhere that there were five hundred miles of bookshelves in the Library of Congress. I wondered how many miles of cooked macaroni were in a single box. How many miles of *uncooked* macaroni? I once thought that if I put a piece of uncooked macaroni in my mouth and sucked on it long enough, it would become cooked. I tried it once. It didn't work.

"Maybe I'll call his parents," my mother said. She was talking to me.

"Huh?"

"His *parents.*"

"Whose parents?"

"Kurt What's-his-name." She put her fork down. "What did you say his name was?"

"Kurt Jones."

"Kurt Jones? I thought you said his name was Kurt Johnson." If she already knew what his name was, why did she ask?

"That's because Jones is his middle name," I said. "Kurt Jones Johnson."

"Oh Billy," she sighed. "As if I didn't have enough mishegas to fool with. Your father had to leave us with barely a penny to our names."

I went back to my macaroni and cheese.

"And speaking of not having a penny," she said, "we need to talk about your bar mitzvah."

"What about it?" I said, alarmed. I put my fork down.

This was the first time she had mentioned my bar mitzvah since my father died. I had been scheduled for next spring, at Beth Israel. Because my father was the principal, I got a "single," which meant that I wouldn't have to share the stage with another kid. A "double" was more typical because there were more kids than Saturdays. Having a single was supposed to be an honor but it meant you had to do everything up there. You had to learn all the Hebrew words and you had to memorize all the melodies and then you had to stand in front of hundreds of people and sing into a microphone that amplified every squeak and bad note.

When my father gave me the date last March, I knew it was more than a whole year away, so I didn't worry about it. I figured that if I put it out of my mind, maybe nobody would ever bring it up again and it wouldn't happen. When in July, my father told me I would probably have to start preparing "at some point in the fall," the worry crept into my head, but not a lot, because "at some point in the fall" was months and months away. But when my mother told me in August that I needed to do a "superior" job on my bar mitzvah and that it was very important for my father's "standing," I started worrying about it a lot.

Then my father died. We moved. I started at a new school. Nobody said anything about a bar mitzvah.

"I called Congregation Shir Shalom in Rockville," my mother said. "We're going to go over there on Sunday to meet with their rabbi."

"Why do I have to do this now?" I said.

"Your father would have wanted it."

"How do you know?"

"Please. You know he would have."

I picked up my fork and started spearing some macaroni.

"Maybe I could do it later," I said. "Like when I grow up."

"That's ridiculous."

"But don't grown-ups get bar mitzvahs? Like when Sammy Davis Jr. became Jewish, maybe he had to have a bar mitzvah."

"Billy, you're not Sammy Davis Jr. You're going to have a bar mitzvah."

"But there's not enough time to prepare," I said looking at the table, not meeting her eyes.

"We'll get a Thursday bar mitzvah," she said. "You won't have to do much."

I knew about Thursday bar mitzvahs. They were given to the kids who had something wrong with them.

"Dad wouldn't have wanted me to have a Thursday bar mitzvah," I said.

"Didn't you just finish telling me that you didn't have time to prepare?"

I looked down at my macaroni and cheese. Long squiggly tubes.

"Eat your dinner," she said. "We're going to visit that rabbi and I'm going to call that Kurt Jones Johnson's parents too."

"I'm not hungry," I said. "May I be excused?"

"Suit yourself," she said. "I'm tired of fighting with you."

I went to my room and shut the door behind me. I pulled the Good 'n Fruities from my pocket and ate every single one, shoveling handfuls into my mouth until the box was empty. Then I took out the folded-up piece of paper—the list of the cursed. I wrote *my stupid mother* under the last name, then folded it back up. I stuffed it into the empty Good 'n Fruity box, then buried it in my big box of baseball cards, underneath a bunch of 1969 California Angels.

THE NEXT MORNING at school—between second and third period—I walked up to Kurt Johnson. He leaned against his locker, sucking on a toothpick. He pointed at me, smiling.

"Mr. Belgium!" he said.

Did that mean we were sort of like friends? Like on *Star Trek*, when Captain Kirk calls Dr. McCoy "Bones"?

"Um, how's it going," I said, "man."

"Okay." He looked confused.

"Um . . . ," I said, "I was wondering if you could do me a very small favor."

"Depends."

"It's really no big deal," I said. "If my mom happens to call your house, could your mom or dad tell her I was with you yesterday after school?"

Kurt blinked three times.

"What?" he said.

"And . . . could they tell her that your middle name is Jones?"

"What the fuck are you talking about?"

I repeated it, leaving out the part about the middle name.

"Why would I be hanging out with you?" he said. He wasn't smiling anymore.

"I don't know."

"What did you say we were doing?"

"I said we were at the Rockville Library working on an extra-credit project."

"Are you fucking serious?"

"Yes," I said. "Sort of."

"So is she going to call my house? Is that what you're saying?"

"She . . . might."

"She . . . *might*? And what if she talks to my asshole old man and says we were at the Fuckville Library studying together? Do you think he's gonna believe that?"

He looked at me. His teeth were a dull brown and I could smell cigarette smoke on him.

"Well, do you?" he asked.

"No."

"No. And he'll be up my ass for some shit I didn't even do. Thanks a lot, dickwad."

"Maybe she won't call," I squeaked. Johnson grabbed me. His fingers felt like steel rods, strong enough to twist my head off like a bottle cap. My head would roll down the stairs while my body wandered through the hallways without a hall pass.

The bell for third period rang.

"Remind me to kick your ass, Blumberg." He pushed me away and walked off.

I SAT IN THIRD-PERIOD ENGLISH, not paying attention. I had never been beaten up before. I had never even been in a fight. At West Montgomery, you got automatically suspended for fighting. I could understand getting suspended for winning a fight, or at least getting in a few good punches. But getting beaten up *and* suspended seemed like double jeopardy. I wasn't sure—technically—what constituted "fighting." If I tried to throw a single punch and missed—would that be a fight? If I raised my arm to block his punches, would that be a fight? What if I closed my eyes and thought about spiritual stuff during the actual beating? *Peace*, I would say as his fist crashed into my mouth, *love*, as he slammed me onto the hard asphalt, *understanding*, as his foot stomped on top of my quivering body. *Peace, love, and understanding*. They couldn't suspend me for that, could they?

The bell rang ending third period. I walked through the hallway toward my next class. I was going to be beaten up and nothing else mattered. I wasn't walking, I was floating. I felt an inner calm. Maybe this was what it was like to be a spirit floating through the air, realizing you'd just died and nothing else matters.

I saw Julie Baines coming toward me with a couple of her girlfriends. She looked at me and smiled, then said something to one of her friends. My God, was the word out already? Maybe she would watch. At the end of my beating, she would have tears in her eyes because she felt so sorry for me. She would kneel down and cradle my head in her lap and gently wipe the blood off my nose and swollen lips. *You okay?* she would ask me—in the same way she asked me if I was okay after the Team Belgium catastrophe. But this time I would be nicer. I would say, spitting out teeth, *not really, but thanks for asking.*

"MR. BELGIUM!" It was Johnson, standing in front of the trophy case, his long thick index finger of steely death pointing at me. He was shaking his head, scowling. I couldn't believe it. Now? I thought he'd wait at least until lunch period, when fights usually happened outside in the parking lot.

I wasn't floating anymore. I was shaking.

Johnson stretched his arms out in front of him, joined his hands, and cracked his knuckles. Over his right shoulder I could see—in the trophy case—a framed picture of a smiling group of kids. *Honor Roll, 1969*, it said. This was the last thing I would see before getting beaten up.

"I'm ready," I said.

"Shut up," he said. "So . . . where were you really?"

"What?"

"Yesterday after school. If you weren't at the library, where were you?"

"Nowhere."

He squeezed the back of my neck with that steel grip.

"Where were you, *really*?" He let go.

I took a deep breath.

"My sixth-grade teacher invited me to her apartment."

Kurt's bushy eyebrows went up. "Seriously?"

"Seriously."

"Why?"

"I don't know. She likes me, I guess."

"What does your sixth-grade teacher look like?"

"I don't know."

"Is she as good looking as Mrs. Dobson?" Mrs. Dobson was one of the typing teachers. I had never actually seen her, but heard that she was the best-looking teacher at West Montgomery.

"I don't know."

"What do you mean you don't know? Either she is or she isn't!"

"Actually," I said, "she's *better* looking than Mrs. Dobson."

"Oh, man! And she invited you to her apartment?"

"Yes."

"Why?"

"Why what?"

He tightened his grip. "Don't fuck with me. Why did she invite you to her apartment?"

"I don't know. She said she wanted to show me something."

"You mean, like, her pussy?"

"Well actually, she did have a cat," I said. "She called it The Black Cat after the Edgar Allan Poe story but it was brown which she said was really ironic because . . ."

"Jesus Christ! I don't want to hear about some fucking cat! Don't you know anything?"

"Not really," I said. The fourth-period bell rang.

I SAT IN FOURTH PERIOD, not paying attention. On a piece of notebook paper, I wrote out my list of Official Worries. I put them in categories. Red Alerts were the things I was most worried about. Kurt Johnson would beat me up because I lied about

Ms. Marvin being better looking than Mrs. Dobson. My mom would call Kurt Johnson's house and find out I was at Ms. Marvin's after school. My mom would scream at Ms. Marvin and Ms. Marvin would scream back and my mom would find out that both me *and my dad* had been to her apartment.

Next were Yellow Alerts. I would get a D in social studies. I wouldn't make the Honor Roll. I was going to have a Thursday bar mitzvah. My tooth was hurting a little, and if the pain got worse, I'd have to tell my mom and go to the dentist.

Finally, there were the Silent Invisible Alerts, always lurking in my head. I didn't have any friends. I missed my dad. And I guessed I kind of hated my mom.

I tried to figure out "the bright side." Everybody was always saying "look at the bright side, look at the bright side." I could only think of three bright sides. First, they now had Good 'n Fruities at 7-Eleven. Two, I didn't know what Mrs. Dobson looked like, and maybe Ms. Marvin actually *was* better looking than Mrs. Dobson and I hadn't lied to Kurt Johnson. And three, maybe my tooth would stop hurting all by itself.

The bell rang ending fourth period. Lunchtime.

I stood in front of my locker. It took five tries before I could get the combination lock to open. I decided to add "Extreme difficulty with combination lock" to the Yellow Alerts. I took out my lunch, a brown paper bag soggy and spotted with tuna fish oil.

I went down the main staircase, down to the typing classrooms to get a look at Mrs. Dobson. I poked my head around the edge of the doorway and saw a teacher talking to some kid. The nameplate on the desk said "Mrs. Dobson" and she was about a *thousand* times better looking than Ms. Marvin. She kind of looked like Barbara Eden from *I Dream of Jeannie*. A genie whose name was Jeannie. Was that irony? I walked back up the steps to the cafeteria. It probably didn't matter that Mrs. Dobson was better looking than Ms. Marvin, because there was no way Kurt Johnson would ever possibly meet Ms. Marvin anyway. Wasn't that a bright side?

I sat at a lunch table, alone, my eyes fixed on the lunch my mom had packed for me: tuna salad on soggy white bread, a baggie of stale Fritos, a bruised banana. She had written on the bag, *If Found Return To: Billy Blumberg, Seventh Grade, West Montgomery Junior High School.* My dad used to tell a story about when he was in the third grade, and there was a kid in his class whose parents owned a delicatessen. One day their lunches got mixed up, and my dad opened the paper bag and found—instead of peanut butter and jelly—a delicious corned beef sandwich and a half-sour pickle. He said it was the best lunch of his whole life because it was something he wasn't expecting.

Kurt Johnson stood across the cafeteria, looking at me. He was smiling. Now what? He came over to me.

"You don't mind if I sit here, do you?" he said, sitting down across from me.

"No," I said. "Want a Frito?"

"What's her name?" he said.

"Whose name?"

"Your sixth-grade teacher."

"Ms. Marvin."

"What's her *first* name?"

"Nancy."

"Nancy." He nodded. "Nice. So . . . Nancy invited you over to show you something. What did Nancy show you?"

"Um," I said. "Well, she showed me this ice cream with little pieces of bubble gum in it. It was really stupid."

"You shitting me?"

"No! She really bought me that ice cream! Actually that was before we got to her apartment."

"Then what did you do when you got there? At her apartment?"

"I don't know. We just talked and stuff. She kind of lit some candles."

"Why?"

"I don't know. She likes candles."

Kurt shifted in his seat. He looked irritated.

"Did she show you her bedroom?"

"Well, no, but she went *into* her bedroom and closed the door."

"For real? Did she take her clothes off?"

"I'm not sure. The door was closed. But I *did* hear the bed-springs creaking."

"Oh, man!" He took a bag of peanuts from his pocket and spilled out a few onto the table.

"Actually," I said, taking a couple of peanuts, "I think she kind of wanted me to come into her bedroom, but it was getting late and I was afraid my mom would think I had been kid-napped and she would call the cops who would have definitely put out an all-points bulletin on me." I popped a peanut into my mouth. "So I had to bolt."

Kurt nodded. "She *definitely* wanted you to come into her bedroom."

I nodded. "Probably. But what could I do? I had to leave. And that's why I asked if you could say you were with me at the library in case my mom calls your house."

"Shit, man, don't worry about that," he said. "I got it cov-ered."

"Cool," I said.

"So when are you going back?" he said.

"Probably never."

"Oh, man! Why the fuck not?"

"Well . . . it's just that she's kind of crazy."

"You mean like a sex maniac?"

"I don't know," I said. "Maybe."

"Listen to me. You have to go back. And—shit—maybe next time you can take me with you."

Was he joking?

"That might not be such a good idea," I said carefully. "She's a teacher and she knows teachers here. She knows Mr. Wilson. You'll get in so much trouble."

"Then why aren't you in 'so much trouble?'"

"I don't know," I said. "Maybe I am."

THE FOLLOWING SUNDAY, my mother and I went to meet with the rabbi at Shir Shalom about my Thursday bar mitzvah. He was a thin bald guy with glasses—all smiles. The top half of his office door was a smoky glass panel with his name, Rabbi Weinberg, printed across in big block letters. He showed us in and motioned us to two chairs facing his desk.

"Welcome, welcome!" he said, settling into his chair. "Welcome to Congregation Shir Shalom!" He had a booming voice, like a radio announcer.

He smiled at my mother, then winked at me. "I'll bet you can tell me what 'shalom' means, Billy."

"Hello, goodbye, and peace," I said.

"Absolutely correct!" he said. He cleared his throat, then said to me, "So I understand you've just moved to Rockville and you need a place to get bar mitzvahed."

"I guess so."

Then to my mother, with furrowed brow. "You said on the phone your husband passed away recently. I'm very sorry."

"Yes. He was a Hebrew school principal and . . ."

"Really? That's wonderful."

". . . and I know he would have wanted Billy to get bar mitzvahed."

"Of course," he said. "As do you, I'm sure."

"I know it's very last minute for scheduling this," she said, "but as I said on the phone we're willing to do a Thursday bar mitzvah. Those are always available, aren't they?"

"Generally, yes," he said, waving his hands. "We can talk about that in a minute."

He looked at me.

"So, Billy, where did you move from?"

My mother looked at me.

"Silver Spring," I said.

"Silver Spring, Maryland?"

"Yes."

He turned to her. "If I may inquire, why isn't your son getting bar mitzvahed at the congregation where your husband was Hebrew school principal?"

"We're never going back there," she said. "After what they did to him."

"What did they do to him?"

"Trust me, Rabbi. You don't want to know."

How embarrassing. Didn't she realize that all these rabbis knew each other? He was probably friends with our old rabbi. They probably had meetings—just like teachers—and instead of talking about students they talked about people like my mother.

"If I may inquire further, which congregation in Silver Spring did you belong to?"

"Beth Israel."

"Beth Israel!" Rabbi Weinberg said, shaking his head sadly. Now he seemed to understand. "Such a tragedy! So unexpected."

"What can I say? Life goes on," my mother said. The rabbi blinked a couple of times, then looked at me.

"Did you know Lawrence?" he said in a hushed sorrowful voice.

"Who?"

"The Feinbaum boy."

"Yes, I know him." I shrugged. So what?

He studied my face. He glanced at my mother. "You don't know, do you?" he said.

"Know what?" my mother said.

He rummaged through a stack of papers on his desk and pulled out the City Life section of the *Washington Post*. He handed the newspaper to my mother, then reached across the desk and pointed at the article:

FATHER AND SON KILLED IN CAR CRASH

I leaned over my mother's shoulder and read:

Harold Feinbaum and his son, Lawrence, were killed Friday evening when a DC Transit bus crossed the center line on East-West Highway and struck their vehicle head on. Both father and son were pronounced dead at the scene.

"OH MY GOD," my mother said. Her face was drained pale.

"Horrible," the rabbi said. "Just horrible."

I didn't say anything.

Harold Feinbaum, Lawrence Feinbaum.

My tooth hurt, worse than ever.

. 6 .

I Can't Explain It

ON THE CAR RIDE HOME, we stopped at a traffic light and my mother sighed from the front seat. "Life goes on," she said, clucking her tongue. She had clucked her tongue over and over in the rabbi's office. She had shaken her head sorrowfully, said *such a tragedy, such a shock* about three or four times, then went ahead and booked my Thursday bar mitzvah.

I sat in the back seat and pondered. If being on the hex list meant bad things would happen to you, then wouldn't *not* being on the list mean that bad things would *not* happen? And yet, the newspaper was full of other people who died, and none of them were on my list. Did that mean I was mathematically eliminated from being responsible for Lawrence and Harold Feinbaum being killed in a car crash?

I fished my hand through the seat cushion crack, searching for the seat belt buckle. Where was it? I pulled out a couple of stale Cheerios, a pencil, an old Life Savers wrapper. Lawrence Feinbaum was the first kid I knew who actually died. One time in the second grade at Hebrew school, he said he'd give me a piece of bubble gum if I promised to stick it under the desk after I chewed it.

"But my dad is the principal," I said.

"But my dad is the *principal*," he said, laughing. He was always laughing at somebody. Now he was a dead body, all cut up and mangled, just lying there. And if it could happen to him, it could happen to me. What if I was on someone else's hex list?

But then, the accident was probably a coincidence, wasn't it? East-West Highway was all curvy and hilly. Cars went really fast and probably careened into each other all the time. The Feinbaums lived somewhere in Chevy Chase, and wasn't it a fact that most fatal car accidents happen near the victim's own home?

I found the buckle and snapped myself in. I still sat in the back seat when my mother drove, even though I had started sitting in the front with my father at the wheel. Like, for example, on that ride home from Hebrew school after Lawrence Feinbaum hit him in the yarmulke with the paper airplane. I had sat in the front passenger seat, staring out the side window. He talked to me about defensive driving, how you have to be ready for anything, and then he said that you have to ask yourself—and these were his exact words—"what if oncoming traffic careens into my lane?"

"You just never know," my mother said, as we pulled into our apartment building's parking lot. Cluck, cluck, cluck.

I WENT UP TO MY ROOM and closed the door. I looked at a copy of *Mad Magazine* lying on my bed, the "Special Polluted Issue" where Alfred E. Neuman grins in a greenish cloud of polluted air. What, me worry? I was mathematically eliminated, just like the Senators were every August. There was no mathematical chance that they would win the pennant, just like there was no chance I killed Harold and Lawrence Feinbaum. But . . . how *did* Uri Geller bend those spoons and guess the contents of those sealed envelopes? My mother said it was all baloney and that metal was metal, but even she wasn't able to explain the unexplainable. My father believed in the spiritual world and now he himself was a spirit. Ms. Marvin said that he would "intercede" on my behalf "in order to enact the hexes." She was the one who suggested I put Harold and Lawrence Feinbaum on the list. I should have said no. My father didn't care for the Feinbaums, but it was hard to believe he would cause them to die horrible deaths. He hated violence. Sometimes when we watched a cowboy or a secret agent getting beaten up or shot on television, he would shake his head and say, *Is this necessary?*

Oh my God, *yes*, I would tell him, *yes*, it was absolutely positively necessary because otherwise the show would be really boring. Who wants to watch a bunch of cowboys or secret agents sit around and solve their problems by having conversations? Why couldn't he understand that? I pulled the Good 'n Fruity box from the baseball cards in my closet. My hands were shaking, my heart racing. I opened the cardboard flap and pulled out the folded-up piece of notebook paper.

This was it.

If the names *Harold Feinbaum* and *Lawrence Feinbaum* had mysteriously disappeared from the list, then I had scientific proof that the spirits were real.

I closed my eyes.

I unfolded the list.

I opened my eyes.

Bob Short
Brooks Robinson
Michael Strohman

Mr. Pappas
Kurt Johnson
Bob King
~~*Julie Baines*~~
Stephen Danielson
Harold Feinbaum
Lawrence Feinbaum
my stupid mother

What a relief. I went back and picked up the *Mad Magazine*. On the cover it said, "In this issue we contaminate *Love Story*." I decided to read it for the third time. My favorite part was when Ryan O'Neal asks Ali MacGraw what her last name is and she says it's "Cowsnowski-Bumstein-Pastafoozala."

I put down the magazine, remembering what Ms. Marvin told me. All this spiritual stuff wasn't like some stupid movie, she had said. This was the real thing. And if there were real spirits like my dad, wouldn't they have better things to do—like staring into the face of God? Why would they waste their time erasing ballpoint-pen ink on a piece of notebook paper stuffed in an empty Good 'n Fruity box and buried under a pile of baseball cards?

I heard a knock on my bedroom door.

"Time for bed," my mother said. *My stupid mother*. Why did I have to add her to the list? Maybe it wouldn't count since I added it after the hexes were enacted. Besides, what if my father's spirit was behind all this. He wouldn't do anything to her, would he?

I quickly folded up the list, stuffed it back into the Good 'n Fruity box, and buried it once again under my baseball cards. My eye caught a 1971 Brooks Robinson. He stood stiffly in his batting stance, grinning at the camera.

I sat down on my bed and finished reading the *Love Story* satire. I reached the end, where Ali MacGraw is in the hospital and the doctor says she's dying of "old movie disease"—because she's looking more and more beautiful as she gets closer to kicking the bucket.

My mom knocked again and stuck her head in, frowning. She looked tired. "How many times do I have to tell you? Go to sleep."

I turned off the light, laid down, and closed my eyes. What would happen? Who would live and who would die? Would there be a 1972 Brooks Robinson card?

THE NEXT MORNING I sat in social studies class as Mr. Pappas lectured us about the branches of government. I watched Julie Baines, two aisles to my right, one row up. If I looked at her sideways around the edge of my glasses, there were two of her, like identical twins. It wasn't her fault she screwed up the Team Belgium oral presentation. I should have tutored her. I would have been patient and kind. She would have been so grateful.

She turned her head and our eyes met. A quarter of a smile flickered on her face and she looked away.

Maybe one day I would tell her I took her off the list and spared her from a horrible curse. *Thanks, Billy*, she would say, awestruck with gratitude. She would say my name a lot. *Billy. Billy. Billy.*

Mr. Pappas stopped talking and frowned at the class. He wanted to know what "bicameral" meant.

"Kurt Johnson," he said. "Why don't you share your knowledge with the rest of us?"

Kurt shrugged and stared at his desk. Pappas wrote *bicameral* on the blackboard. When he got to the letter "l" his chalk snapped and he banged his hand against the blackboard. *God-dammit*, he said, shaking his hand. He sucked on his knuckle. Then he opened his desk drawer and took out a Band-Aid. He put it on, as we watched. This was the highlight of the class, by far. Then he turned back toward us.

"BI-CAM-ER-AL," he said. "We're waiting, Mr. Johnson."

"Uh," Kurt said, "buy cameras?"

Poor Kurt. I should have taken him off the list, too. He was my best friend at this stupid school. I looked around the room. Kurt Johnson, Bob King, and Stephen Danielson. Team Belgium. They weren't so bad. They didn't deserve this. If only they had done a little bit of work.

"It would behoove you people to read the assignments," Mr. Pappas shouted at us. His eyes scanned the room, going from kid to kid, the same way my dad used to do it. When he got to me, I saw a hesitation, a flicker of doubt, and then he looked away, still shaking his banged-up knuckle.

The bell rang. I walked up to Kurt as he was gathering up his stuff.

"Buy cameras," I said in a loud voice. "That's a good one, man."

Kurt smiled, but it wasn't a friendly smile. "How's Nancy?"

"Okay, I guess." Out of the corner of my eye, I saw Julie Baines walking out of the room.

"Your mom hasn't called my house."

"Maybe she won't call."

"Don't worry. I've got it all taken care of."

"Thanks," I said. "I appreciate that."

"You should."

I nodded. "I definitely appreciate it."

"Don't you worry about a thing. You look worried. Are you worried?"

"I'm not worried."

"Shit, man, you *always* look worried."

"I do?"

"You need to relax, man. Release some tension. Know what I mean?"

"I think so."

He laughed.

"Say hello to Nancy for me."

AFTER SCHOOL I went to the 7-Eleven. I saw Julie Baines smoking a cigarette, sitting by herself on a cement ledge next to the parking lot. I'd seen her sitting there before, always with another girl and two guys. Now she was sitting by herself and she looked sad, staring into the distance. I started walking into the 7-Eleven, then stopped and thought about it. Should I go up to her and say hello? I had taken her name off the list. But did I really look worried all the time? That probably wasn't attractive to girls. On the other hand maybe looking worried meant that I was sensitive, and on that TV show *Love, American Style*, the girls always say they like sensitive guys. I eased by her slowly. She might say *hello*, and I'd say *hello there, Julie, how are you?*

She didn't say hello. I walked into the 7-Eleven and bought three boxes of Good 'n Fruities. I told myself that if she was still sitting there when I left the store I would go up to her. I left the 7-Eleven, sort of hoping she would be gone. Then it would be out of my hands. What was I supposed to do, follow her around? But she was still there.

"Hey," I said.

"Hey," she whispered, barely looking at me. It was like someone had died.

I just stood there. "I'm sorry about the Team Belgium thing."

She sighed. "I don't care about that."

"Where are your friends?"

"They're not my friends."

She looked at me, her eyes shiny with tears.

"What happened?" I asked.

"I don't want to talk about it," she said, adding, "with you."

She stared past me, at the traffic on Route 355. Should I leave? I looked around, then saw the Sunday newspaper sitting in a trash can.

"Do you want to see something?"

She shrugged. "I don't care."

I picked up the paper and pulled out the City Life section.

"See this article?" I pointed to "Father and Son Killed in Car Crash."

She looked at it. "So?"

"So I knew them when I lived in Silver Spring. That kid. And his father too."

"Really? Was the kid a friend of yours?"

"Not really. But I used to see him all the time."

"And now he's dead," she said in a flat voice. "We'll all be dead some day. Nothing really matters."

"That's so true." I held out the box of Good 'n Fruities. "Want one?"

"No," she said. "Those things are gross."

"You're right. Good 'n Plenties are much better."

She looked at me. "You don't really think that. Stand up for yourself, Billy."

Billy. "You're right," I said. "I'll do that."

She took a puff on her cigarette and threw the butt on the ground. Then she lit another one. She kept staring straight ahead, at people parking, car doors slamming. She could get up and leave at any moment.

"You know that car crash in the newspaper?"

She took a puff and nodded.

"I might have caused it."

She blew out some smoke and looked at me. "How?"

"Well, I can't really talk about it."

She shrugged and turned back away from me.

"All right, I'll tell you. But you can't tell anyone."

"Okay."

"Promise?"

"Yeah, whatever."

I looked around. More cars parking. Birds squawking. Puffy clouds floating in the sky.

"They were cursed," I said. "I went to a séance and I got some creepy lady to put their names on a hex list. But I didn't mean for anything like this to happen."

"How do you know it wasn't a coincidence?"

"Maybe it was and maybe it wasn't. But did you see what happened with Pappas today?"

"He yelled at us. He does that every day."

"Yes, but he hurt his hand against the blackboard, remember? And guess what? I put Pappas on that same list!"

"But hitting your hand on a stupid blackboard is not like dying in a car crash."

"You don't understand how it works," I said. "A hex can be anything bad. Big or little."

She nodded.

"If Pappas hitting his hand on the blackboard wasn't the actual curse, what do you think will happen to him?"

"It could be anything," I said. "Maybe his vocal cords will get all paralyzed in class and he'll start whimpering like a little puppy."

"That would be cool," she said, smiling for the first time. "If that happens, I'll totally believe you."

She took a long puff on her cigarette and blew out the smoke.

"So . . . who else is on the list?" she asked.

"I shouldn't say," I said. "It's bad luck to tell someone who's on the list."

"But you already told me Pappas."

"Right. I did."

She threw her cigarette butt onto the asphalt and ground it in with her shoe.

"Can you add people to the list?"

"I don't know. Maybe." She was looking at me, eyebrows raised. "I guess so," I said.

"So where is it?"

"Where is what?"

"The *list*."

"In my closet. In my room."

"Can you show it to me?"

"I don't know," I said. "Maybe."

She looked at me with this weird smile.

"When do you want to see it?" I asked.

"How about now?"

"You want me to go get it and come back here?"

"Don't be stupid," she said. "I'll come with you. Is your mom home?"

WE WALKED TO MY APARTMENT and she started talking to me, really fast, like we were friends. She told me about John and Marla, her "ex-friends," how she knew Marla ever since kindergarten, how they met John in the seventh grade, how she used to think he was really cool, and how when she saw John and Marla kissing next to Julie's own locker, she decided to hate them forever.

We stood at the traffic light in front of my apartment building.

"They were kissing in front of your locker?" I asked, watching for cars. "Right in front of you?"

"Right in front of the whole world."

I felt really bad for her. "The exact same kind of thing happened to me once," I said.

"This way?" she asked, pointing toward my building. She walked out into the street even though the light hadn't changed. I followed her.

"You should put John and Marla on your hex list," she said as she stepped onto the opposite curb. "Maybe they'll go skiing together and they'll be in the ski lift, and the cable will snap, and then as they fall to the ground they'll look at the glass and see their reflection and understand in that one second how they've betrayed me."

"That could happen," I said. "Or maybe they'll go to Hawaii to see the volcanoes, and while they're kissing they'll fall into the lava. Then, five hundred years from now, scientists will find their bodies encased in rock and their mouths will be frozen into this expression nobody can figure out and they'll call in a professional lip-reader and the lip-reader will say, yes, I think I can tell what they're saying—could it be—yes, I think it is—it is the words: 'We're sorry, Julie.'"

She laughed. This was now the longest conversation I'd ever had with a girl I wasn't related to.

"So is your mother named Rosemary?"

"No," I said. "It's Rebecca. Why?"

"Because maybe you're Rosemary's Baby."

I looked at her. "What?"

"Get it?" she asked.

"I got that joke," I said. "I was just pretending I didn't."

"Yeah right," she said, smiling at me. "You're not so smart about everything. Do you know who Rosemary's baby's father is?"

"Rosemary's husband?"

"Nope."

"I've never actually seen that movie."

"It's really *really* creepy. Someday, maybe I'll tell you."

"Okay!" I said. Maybe we would be at a school dance or out on a date—someday—and she would tell me who Rosemary's baby's father was.

We reached the front door of my building. I went in first, but I held the door for her. We passed by the mail room.

"That's the mail room," I said. "If you get a big letter that won't fit in your box, you have to pick it up at the front desk."

"You're the only kid at West Montgomery I know who doesn't live in a house," she said. "Why do you live here?"

"I don't know," I said, pushing the up button on the elevator. "Do you remember that show *Family Affair*? They lived in an apartment."

"Yeah, but they had a butler."

"I wouldn't even *want* a butler," I said. "He would get on my nerves—folding clothes, polishing stuff, hanging around and everything."

We got on the elevator. "Five!" I said, punching the button

hard with my knuckle, like I'd been doing it all my life and it was no big deal for me, but would be a huge deal for anyone not used to living with elevators.

"I used to worry about the elevator cable snapping," I said as we rose. "But if that happened you know what I would do? I would jump up in the air just before it hit the ground."

"So . . ." Julie started, "what if John and Marla were in an elevator in a really tall building . . ."

"The Empire State Building," I said. "Or the Washington Monument if it was local."

"Yeah, and the elevator cord snaps, and . . ."

"And they wouldn't have time to jump up in the air because they'd be busy kissing!"

She didn't laugh at that one. The elevator door opened and we walked down the long hallway.

"It's like a hotel," she said. She wrinkled her face. "Smells like onions."

We got to my front door. I put my right hand in my right pocket. No key. Gone. It must have slipped through a hole in my pocket. It was probably lying on the sidewalk next to the parking lot outside 7-Eleven. I thought I remembered hearing a whispery metal-on-concrete sound. I could see the key in my head, that dull glint flat against the dusty sidewalk. Should I go back and Julie could wait here? Or should we both go back? Or should I go to the front desk and tell them I lost the key, in which case they'd call my mother because there was a $20 fine?

"What's the matter?" Julie said.

I put my left hand in my left pocket. The key! "Nothing," I said. I opened the door and we went inside. A bare sofa, a coffee table, the kitchen table in the corner with two chairs facing each other.

"Home sweet home."

"So your mom's at work?"

"Yes."

"Rosemary," she said, teasing.

"Rebecca."

"What does she do?"

"Works for some insurance company."

"What does your dad do?"

I put the key back in my right pocket, where it belonged.

"He travels a lot," I said, finally.

She looked at me, kind of strange.

"Where does he travel to?"

"All over," I said. "Want to see my room?"

My room was a mess, puzzles and games on the floor, my dresser drawers open, T-shirts and underwear flopping out.

"Geez. Looks like my little brother's room," Julie said, her nose crinkly like it was when she said the hallway smelled like onions.

"Do you like *Mad Magazine*?" I picked up the Special Polluted Issue, splayed open on my bed.

"I don't know."

I showed her the *Love Story* satire, the part where Ali MacGraw says her name is "Cowsnowski-Bumstein . . . Pastafoozala."

"Why is that funny?"

"I can't explain it," I said. "It just is."

"Where's the hex list? I want to see it."

I once watched an episode of *Love, American Style* where the guy invited the girl to his "pad" to see his etchings. The plan was to show her the etchings and then they would start kissing. I knelt in front of my box of baseball cards on the closet floor.

If breakfast without orange juice was like a day without sunshine, then . . . my hex list was like the etchings and maybe Julie would start kissing me when I showed her the list. I decided to just let whatever happened happen.

"My little brother collects baseball cards," she said, as I started rooting around in the pile.

"I don't really collect them anymore," I lied. "These are just my old ones that I use for camouflage." I pulled the Good 'n Fruity box out of the baseball cards.

"It's in here," I said.

"Why do you keep the hex list in a box of candy?"

"I'm not sure," I said. "I can't explain it." I opened the cardboard flap and pulled out the folded-up piece of notebook paper.

"Are you ready?"

"Yes," she said. "I'm ready."

"Are you sure?"

"Yeah. Give it."

I handed her the hex list. On that episode of *Love, American Style* there were three different girls. The first one hated the etchings and slapped the guy in the face. The second girl recognized one particular etching from when she was a little kid, and it turned out she was his long-lost half-sister. The third girl liked the etchings, but then my mother came in and said I had to turn off the TV and go to bed, so I never found out what happened.

I handed Julie the list. She opened it and read it. Then her mouth fell open. She looked at me, frowning.

"What's this?"

"What's what?"

"Why would you put my name on the list?"

"But I had your name crossed out."

"But why did you put it on in the first place?"

"Well . . . it was the Team Belgium project."

"That stupid thing? Who cares? Why would you want something horrible to happen to me just because of *that*? You don't even know me!"

"I can't expl. . ."

"People on this list actually died!"

"Not all of them."

"*Two* of them!"

"Well, sort of."

"What do you mean 'sort of'? You showed me the article. They're not 'sort of' dead. They're *dead* dead."

"*Sort of* meaning I'm not sure it was because of the list. It might have been a coincidence."

She shook her head and walked out of my room. I followed after her. She headed for the front door.

"But I took you off the list!"

"This is really creepy."

"Don't go."

"Really really creepy."

"But you're the one who wanted to put John and Marla on the list!" I pointed out.

"That's different," she said, opening the door.

I couldn't see how it was different. I didn't know what happened with the girl who liked the etchings. And I hadn't figured out the identity of Rosemary's baby's father. I didn't understand any of it.

. 7 .

Brooks Robinson

IN JULY MY FATHER had taken me to a baseball game. He seemed happy that summer, but I didn't know what he had to be happy about. He was in trouble at work and he had to beg Harold Feinbaum and the rabbi for his job when Hebrew school started up again in September. He fought with my mother a lot. And as if that wasn't enough, it was announced that the Washington Senators were moving to Irving, Texas, after the season to become something called "the Texas Rangers."

"Texas?" he said, at dinner the day it was announced. "Why don't they just move the Washington Monument to a cow pasture in Iowa?"

"Why would you name a team after a bunch of stupid park rangers?" I said. "Do they even have parks in Texas? Do they even have trees?"

"It's not that kind of rangers," he said. "They're crazy policemen who wear cowboy hats."

"Irving, Texas?" I said.

"*Irving*, Texas," he said, laughing. "What kind of name is that?"

"Enough," my mother said. She glared at me, then said to him, "You have more important things to worry about."

A week later, he asked me if I wanted to go to a baseball game. We had gone to one or two Senators games a year in previous seasons, and we hadn't yet been to one this summer.

"Definitely," I said. "I can't believe they're leaving forever."

"I'm not talking about a Senators game," he said. "We're going up to Baltimore."

Was he kidding? We hated the Orioles. They were the best team in baseball. The Senators were the worst. The Orioles not only always beat the Senators, they humiliated them. My father had liked to say that rooting for the Orioles was like rooting for General Motors, and that rooting for the Orioles against the Senators was like rooting for the Babylonians against the Jews during the destruction of the First Temple in 586 BC.

"Why aren't we seeing the Senators?" I asked.

"Look to the future, not the past," he said. "The Senators should be dead to you."

"But they're still playing."

"Granted, the body is still warm," he said. "A lifeless body, nevertheless."

"But they're my favorite team."

"They have forsaken you. Why should you not forsake them?"

"I'm loyal."

"Were they loyal to you? Why not open your heart to a new team?" His eyes gleamed. "A team of champions!"

We drove to Baltimore on a Sunday afternoon. I had to admit that Memorial Stadium was a lot cooler than RFK Stadium, where the Senators played. In Memorial Stadium, you could see the windows of people's houses over the center-field hedges. From our seats in the upper deck behind home plate, I had to admit how great it would be to live in one of those houses. I could watch games from my bedroom window with binoculars. Or, I could watch games on TV, and if someone hit a ball out of the park, I would rush outside and see that very same ball carom off the street and bounce up my front steps.

"That would be better than living anywhere else in the world," I said, pointing to those houses, "except for maybe the houses across the street from Disneyland."

"You think so? Disneyland would get tedious, believe me," my father said. "The same rides every day, the same trash cans overflowing with paper cups and soggy popcorn boxes, the same poor schmoes wandering around, sweating like pigs inside flannel cartoon suits with fake smiles painted on their faces."

"Sounds pretty good to me," I said, eating popcorn from a non-soggy popcorn box. The usual rule at baseball games was I could get one Coke, one sugary thing, and one salty thing. Either all together or separately in any order I chose. But this baseball game was not like any other baseball game. I was up to two cotton candies, three popcorns, two Cokes. I was allowed to get as much as I wanted, except I still wasn't allowed to get a hot dog because it had pork in it.

It was the fifth inning and Brooks Robinson, the Orioles' all-star third baseman, was leading off. My father focused his binoculars on home plate.

"I *hate* him," I said.

"Why?"

"I hate the way he fidgets around when he's at bat."

"Okay," he said. "And by that, I mean, okay I understand what you're saying, not okay I approve of your position."

He handed me the binoculars. I watched Brooks Robinson swing and miss. Strike two.

"Here's the way I look at it," my father said. "When I root

for a team, I operate inside a moral vacuum. By that I mean, I don't care whether I personally like the players or not, I don't care what kind of human beings they are or what sins they may or may not have committed in their private lives. I only care about what they do to contribute to my team's victory." Ball two.

"So now that you're this big Orioles fan," I said, "if Brooks Robinson was a dirty rotten liar and cheater, you'd still root for him?"

"Yes. I would condemn him in any other societal context, but within the context of baseball, I apply the moral vacuum."

"What if he robbed a bank? What if he murdered someone?"

"In that case, I would condemn him, but only to the extent that he would be in jail and no longer able to help the Orioles continue their winning ways." Ball three.

"What if he murdered someone, and you were the only person who knew about it but you couldn't prove it and you couldn't go to the police? Let's say he never gets caught and he wins the Most Valuable Player award and the Orioles win the World Series. Would you still apply the moral vacuum?"

He sat still for a couple of seconds, thinking.

"Who does he have to murder?" he asked. Called strike three. Through the binoculars, I could see Brooks Robinson's face, grimacing and contorted and angry. The game went on. I ate another cotton candy and a box of popcorn. Finally, it was the bottom of the ninth. The Orioles were losing by one run to the Tigers, but they had runners at first and second with two men out. And, of course, Brooks Robinson was up.

This was it. The Senators were going to be my past, and the Orioles were my future. But I didn't care. I still hated the way

Brooks Robinson fidgeted when he stood at the plate. I hated the way he made those lucky plays at third base, just flopping on the ground like a big clumsy moose, the ball magically sticking in his glove. I hated everything about him and his stupid team.

My father was on his feet with all the other Baltimorons, clapping and stomping. I sat quietly, my view obstructed by the backs of the people standing in front of me. I heard a loud crack and that rising crushing sound from a crowd of thirty thousand. Then wild cheers. Brooks Robinson had hit a home run. Game over, Orioles win again.

"Do you see, Billy?" he said. "Do you see? If this were the Senators, it would have been Ed Brinkman and he would have struck out. Recrimination. Despair. *Losing.* But this is the Orioles. Brooks Robinson hits a home run. Joy. Ecstasy. *Winning.*"

"But Brooks Robinson just *happened* to be at bat. It could have been an Orioles strikeout by Andy Etchebarren, who stinks. It could have been a Senators home run by Frank Howard, who's great."

"It could have been," he said. "But it wasn't."

B. Robinson in Domestic Accident
November 24, 1971

(AP) *Brooks Robinson, all-star third baseman for the Baltimore Orioles, sprained his ankle on a patio deck at his home in Florida, it was reported yesterday. Robinson is expected to be fully recovered by the start of spring training in March, team officials said.*

I cut the article out of the paper and buried it under my baseball cards, next to the hex list. A sprained ankle—not much of a hex. The only reason it was in the paper was because he was the "all-star third baseman for the Baltimore Orioles." Something not newsworthy could have happened to him, and I wouldn't even know about it. He could have bitten his tongue while he was eating a hot dog. He could have lost his favorite ballpoint pen. It could be anything.

I wondered if Julie Baines had seen it. She had seen the list and she knew that Brooks Robinson was on it. What if she freaked out and told everybody at school? But I had nothing to worry about, did I? She had promised not to tell anyone. A promise is a promise, and a sacred trust involving a hex list containing people who have actually died is something that nobody with half a brain would break. But on the other hand, given her performance on Team Belgium, maybe her brain wasn't all that big. Plus, when I asked her to promise, she didn't say *yes, I absolutely promise, so help me God.* She said, *yeah, whatever.*

I knew what to do. I tore out a piece of lined notebook paper and wrote a letter.

Julie,

Please don't tell anyone about the hex list—the one that I showed you because you wanted me to show it to you. I know you promised you wouldn't and that means you probably won't. But I thought you should know that there's a rule about how anyone who breaks a promise involving a hex list will be cursed with a hex. I wish that wasn't the rule, but that's just the way that particular rule happens to be. I'm sorry. I hope you haven't broken your promise by the time you read this.

Yours truly,
Billy Blumberg

I slipped the letter into her locker before homeroom. Writing things out exactly the way you wanted was *so* much more effective than talking to someone face-to-face. How much better would the world be if everyone carried around pens and pads of paper, slipping little notes into each other's lockers or under their front doors? I had nothing to worry about.

But during first-period social studies, I could see I had plenty to worry about. Brooks Robinson had sprained his ankle. Mr. Pappas still had a bandage on his finger, and it looked like a bigger bandage than the one he put on yesterday, meaning a deadly chalk dust infection might be spreading from his finger to the rest of his body. Julie Baines wouldn't look at me and I didn't know if it was because she either had or hadn't read my letter. Maybe it had fallen into a locker crevice and she didn't see it. Kurt Johnson kept staring at me and shaking his head. The rest of Team Belgium—Bob King and Stephen Danielson—were watching me too. Danielson was drawing something with his black Flair pen on a piece of notebook paper. I couldn't see it clearly from a distance, but it looked like either a big moose with floppy ears, or a picture of me smiling like a circus clown, arms and legs limp and dangling, hanging from a noose at the end of a rope.

The day went on. I got more worried. Something was going on. Nobody was talking to me, although—I reassured myself—nobody usually talked to me anyway. Between fifth and sixth period, I saw Julie at her locker by herself. She looked at me, her expression like a blank sheet of rock on the face of a cliff.

"Did you see the letter?" I said.

"What letter?"

"The one I slipped into your locker before homeroom."

"I didn't see any letter."

"Never mind," I said. "It must have fallen into a locker crevice."

"The locker crevice," she said, nodding.

"Did you see the sports page this morning?"

"I don't read the sports page."

She reached into her locker and grabbed a math book. She slammed the locker door and rocketed away, not even looking me in the face. This whole conversation proved—again—why writing was so much better than talking. Of course she didn't read the sports page. She probably didn't know who Brooks Robinson was. Suppose the guy who invented high heels or lipstick had a stroke. I wouldn't know about it because it would be in the *Washington Post*'s Style section.

I felt a big body looming behind me. It was Kurt Johnson, smiling, but not the friendly kind of smiling. Had he seen the sports page this morning?

"So Blumberg," he said. "I heard you put me on some fucking list."

"What list?" I said, weakly. I felt panic bubbling up from my stomach. The letter didn't fall into a locker crevice.

"Not that I believe in some stupid bullshit curse," he said.

"You shouldn't," I said. "That's very smart of you."

He peered at me. "So . . . ," he said slowly, "is it really true that two people on the list died?"

"Sort of," I said. "But it was a coincidence."

"And is it true that you put Pappas on the list right before he split open his finger against the blackboard?"

"No," I said. "First of all, he didn't split his finger open. It was only a small scrape. And second of all, I put his name on a couple of weeks ago when I put all the names on the list."

"Including *my name*?"

"I'm really sorry about that."

"I thought we were buddies. Aren't we buddies?"

"Absolutely we're buddies!"

He sighed loudly.

"What are we going to do about this, Blumberg?"

"I'll take you off the list," I said. "I'll do it first thing when I get home this afternoon."

"You can do that?"

"Sure. I'll just put a line through it. First thing!"

"How do you know it will work?"

"Because I drew a line through Julie Baines's name on the list and nothing happened to her."

"How do you know something won't happen to her tomorrow?"

"Because," I said, thinking hard, "once you draw a line through someone's name the spirits understand that it's the signal to leave that person alone. If you want, I can even blot out your name with white-out. That's even more effective."

"How do the spirits know that's the signal?"

"They just know."

"How?"

"In the Bible, how did the Angel of Death know which houses to skip over when he was killing all the first-born Egyptians?"

"What?"

"Don't you remember? In the book of Exodus, how they marked their houses with lamb's blood?"

Kurt shook his head, disgusted. He took a step toward me.

"I heard that you went to a séance and some creepy lady put a curse on me."

Bubbling panic again. "Yes," I said. "Sort of."

"So if she put on the curse, how are you going to take it off all by yourself?"

"Well, she told me that I had the power to remove it."

"Right," he said, nodding. "Let me ask you something else. When someone has a séance, what do they do? Do they light a candle?"

"Yes, I think so," I said. "Generally speaking."

"So did this lady light a candle at this séance where she put the curse on me?"

"Yes."

"You mean the way you told me that Nancy lit a candle when you visited her?"

"Kind of," I said. "Yes and no. But this was a different lady who did the séance."

"Do you think I'm stupid?"

"No."

"No, what?"

"No, I don't think you're stupid." I was the one who was stupid. I had given him enough clues. He had figured it out. Would the hex now turn on me?

"Thanks, man. That means a lot coming from you. So do you think your sex-maniac girlfriend will remove the curse on me? *Personally?*

"No."

"Why not?"

"Because," I said. My bad tooth was throbbing. "Because . . . she's not my girlfriend and . . . it doesn't work that way."

"Too bad," he said. "Make it work that way."

"But she's a teacher," I said. "You'll get in trouble."

"She's only an elementary school teacher. She can't do shit."

I told Kurt that visiting Ms. Marvin wasn't necessary and

that I would be happy to write a letter asking her to take the curse off him and put new ones on anybody he wanted. I told him she probably had good spells that could give him a million dollars or A's on his report card without doing any work. Spells that would enable him to beat up any seventh, eighth, or ninth grader in the continental United States. Wouldn't that be great? And not only that, but I would write what a great guy Kurt was and how he looked like a young James Bond and how he thought she was prettier than Barbara Eden in *I Dream of Jeannie*. Finally, I would let him read the letter and I would be delighted to make any and all changes he told me to make. He would even be allowed to mail it himself, if he wanted to. It was a fantastic offer, wasn't it?

No," he said. "It's not."

I had two choices. Either I would take him to Ms. Marvin's apartment or he would beat the crap out of me.

CHALK-MARKED SIDEWALKS with weeds growing through the cracks, traffic whizzing by, squashed McDonald's cups crumpled against the curb. Here I was again, wandering the streets of Rockville, only this time I wasn't alone. Kurt walked next to me, his giant fists coiled like snakes in his jacket pockets.

I felt like a kidnapping victim—forced to go out in public, surrounded by potential rescuers, but all too aware that my assailant was at my side with a gun in his pocket aimed right at my heart. I saw a man coming out the Safeway, headed our way. He wore a blue buttoned-up shirt with no tie, looking like somebody's father on his way home. *Help me help me*, I shouted in my mind. If spoon bending could work for Uri Geller, maybe planting thoughts in a stranger's brain could work for me. All he had to do was stop, and say four simple words: *what's going on here?* I stared at him, concentrating hard, but he walked right past us.

I could hear Kurt breathing. He wasn't talking much; it was like he was nervous or worried. I didn't think guys like him got nervous or worried about anything. Was he more worried about getting the curse removed, or nervous because he was about to meet Nancy the sex maniac? It's like if you're starving and freezing to death at the same time. What do you want to do first: eat a hamburger or put on a sweater?

We reached a corner. I could see Ms. Marvin's apartment building a block away.

"That one?" Kurt said, pointing.

We crossed the street.

"I'm not sure we should do this," I said. "You'll get in trouble."

"No I won't," he said. "If anyone's gonna get in trouble, it won't be me."

"What if she's not home?" I asked.

"She better be."

We rounded a corner, right in front of the apartment building. My stomach and tooth were killing me, both at the same time.

"What do I tell her?" I asked.

"Tell her I'm your best friend and you want her to take the curse off of me. That's all you hafta say."

"Okay."

"And then whatever happens happens."

What should I do, I wondered? I could just stop and tell Kurt I changed my mind. What would be worse, seeing Ms. Marvin again or getting beaten up? If I never saw her again, maybe I would stop thinking about why my father felt better last summer and why my mother was so angry at him all the time. If I could stop thinking about that, I could then stop thinking about why he killed himself and whether it was my fault for laughing when the yarmulke flew off his head. And then I could stop thinking about why I hated Rockville and my new school where I didn't have any friends and that I had written "my stupid mother" on the hex list. If I stopped thinking about these things for long enough, all of my big worries, the Red Alert ones, would disappear. And I would achieve my goal of being a normal, happy kid.

On the other hand, I didn't want to get beaten up.

"Here it is," I said. We were in front of the building.

"All these fucking apartment buildings look alike," Kurt said. "I'm glad I live in a real house."

"I used to live in a house too."

We entered the lobby and headed for the elevator.

"What floor?" Kurt said, staring at the up button.

"Seven."

We got on the elevator and he punched the "7" button with his knuckle. Maybe seeing Ms. Marvin again wouldn't be so bad. She wouldn't talk to me about my dad, because Kurt would be there. Then she could remove all the curses. I didn't want anybody else to die or bust their finger or sprain their ankle. Also, since she was friends with Mr. Wilson, she could call him and tell him I'd been shanghaied to her apartment and Kurt would get in huge trouble. Maybe he would even get expelled and I would never have to worry about him again.

The elevator door opened on the seventh floor. This was it. We walked down the long hallway of doors. I wondered how many times my father had walked down this hallway. Did he have an assailant shadowing him too, with a secret gun pointed at his heart?

"Which one is it?" Kurt said.

"Number 714."

"You sure?"

"Yes. Definitely number 714."

708, 710, 712. We stood in front of 714. Kurt pulled me in front of him and made me ring the doorbell. For about five seconds there was silence behind the door. Then I heard footsteps. They got louder. There was a pause and then the lock unclicked.

The door opened. A wiry-haired lady in a flowered robe looked at us, squinting.

"What can I do for you boys?" she said. Maybe she was Ms. Marvin's mother or great-aunt. Maybe she was the head witch in Ms. Marvin's coven.

"Well?" she said.

"Is Ms. Marvin here?" I said.

"Who?"

"Nancy?" I heard Kurt say from behind me.

"Sorry, boys, there's no one here by that name. Maybe you have the wrong apartment."

She closed the door.

"She doesn't live here," I said to Kurt.

"I got ears." He was shaking his head.

"Maybe she moved."

"Yeah, right," he said. He stood close to me, staring me in the face.

"I *know* that 714 is *definitely* the right apartment because 714 is Babe Ruth's all-time home run record. I know every all-time home run leader. Mickey Mantle, 536. Jimmy Foxx, 534. Ted Williams, 521. See? I know all those numbers and it absolutely was apartment 714."

"So where is she?"

"Maybe she was summoned back to the spirit world and she's writing reports about life among the humans and now she's gone and won't be back for a hundred years."

"Uh-huh."

"It will be the year 2071, right? We'll both be dead by then unless they invent pills that make you live forever. Which they won't. So I think we'll probably never see her again. So, you know, what can we do? What can anyone do?"

Kurt said, "I know exactly what we can do."

WE STOOD IN A VACANT LOT. Behind me was the bare back wall of the Safeway, a vast expanse of grayness with a small dirty-white metal door facing a dumpster. To my right was a concrete wall, and to my left, a couple of craggy trees blocking the view from the cars zooming by on Route 355. Around me were tall grass, rocks, weeds, bottles, and trash. My blood would seep in and leave no trace. This is where bigger people took smaller people in order to beat the crap out of them, and this is where Kurt Johnson had taken me.

My only chance was the spirits. Maybe my father could do something. Maybe Kurt would temporarily go blind and I could get away. I saw an empty Good 'n Fruity box at my feet. Was this a sign?

Kurt looked around to see if anyone was watching. Nobody was.

He positioned me in front of him, like he was setting up a golf shot. Then he said, "This is nothing compared to what's going to happen to you if anything fucking happens to me." He pushed me, and I staggered back toward the wall.

"If you beat me up," I said. "The hex might be worse."

"Why?" He pushed me again.

"My father is watching over me. He's responsible for the hex and you don't want to get him mad."

"Your old man?" he said, looking around. "I don't see him. Where the hell is he?"

"He's an invisible spirit."

"What do you mean, an invisible spirit? You told me he was a traveling salesman." He pushed me again.

"I lied. He was a Hebrew school principal in Silver Spring. He killed himself."

"No shit? How did he kill himself?"

Nobody came out of the dirty-white metal door, nobody poked their head through the trees. Kurt was not going to go blind.

"Fuck you," I said.

"Asshole," he said, driving his fist into my stomach.

I doubled over, gasping for breath. The pain was incredible. He straightened me up, then pushed me hard against the Safeway wall. *Help*, I cried out. *Shut the fuck up*, Kurt said. On the other side of that wall, maybe somebody's mom was selecting a package of ground beef for supper. She was going to make a meatloaf. She couldn't hear me.

I might as well fight back, I figured, even though it would be like the Senators trying to beat the Orioles. I threw a punch and it glanced off his shoulder. He hit me in the mouth. I could taste blood and tears were gathering in my eyes. I threw another punch and my half-formed fist stung against his forearm.

If my father *was* watching, I might as well impress him by not crying, by fighting back. Maybe he would gather his spirit buddies to watch and he would compare me to that great Jewish martyr he always talked about—Rabbi Akiva, who was tortured by the Romans. I swung again, this time landing a solid blow on Kurt's nose. He staggered backward and snorted like an angry elephant. Then he hit me on the jaw, and I saw a flash of light. I fell to the ground. I closed my eyes and heard myself moaning.

"Next time don't fuck with me," Kurt said. I heard his footsteps getting fainter. He was gone.

I lay among the weeds and rocks and bottles. Rabbi Akiva, whose flesh they tore off with hot iron forks.

Hello, Dad? I whispered.

I felt a cold raindrop on my cheek.

If you could smite the Feinbaums, maul Pappas's finger, and make a twelve-time all-star third baseman sprain his ankle on a patio in Florida, how hard would it be to look out for me?

. 8 .

Labor Day Weekend

WE ALWAYS HAD BAKED CHICKEN on Friday nights. But on my father's last Labor Day weekend there was something new.

"Sweet and sour meatballs," my mother said, unveiling the covered dish before our raised eyebrows.

"Interesting," he said.

"I got the recipe from the newspaper. I wanted to try something different."

"And I commend you for that."

"Thanks—that means a lot," she said. "Coming from you." She ladled a few meatballs onto his plate, then onto mine. They sat in a reddish brownish greenish sauce.

"I can taste the sweet," he said, taking a mouthful. "What did you put in these meatballs?"

"Grape jelly."

"It's not altogether unpleasant," he said, putting his fork down. "But it violates the eleventh commandment. Thou shalt not mix the sweet and the savory."

His eyes twinkled. Hers didn't. He turned to me. "The sweet and the savory and never the twain shall meet!" he proclaimed. "Does one slather chocolate sauce over spaghetti? Do you pour maple syrup on a hot dog? No, you do not!"

"I heard there's this restaurant in Colorado?" I said. "Where somebody put LSD in the salt shakers!"

"I'm not sure that's the sweet and the savory," he said thoughtfully. "Is LSD sweet to the taste? I wouldn't know."

"What kind of sick person would put hard drugs in a salt shaker?" my mother said.

"Some crazy hippie," said my father. "Can you imagine?"

"Nobody says 'hippie' anymore," I pointed out.

"What do they say?"

"Unemployed," my mother said.

My father looked straight at me, gulping down another mouthful and shaking his head in mock seriousness.

"The sweet . . . ," he said, ". . . *and the savory*! The young and the restless! The yin and the yang!

"Look," she said. "You don't have to eat it."

"The sweet and the savory," I said. "The Flintstones and the Jetsons. The Cokes and the Pepsi's."

"The sorrow and the pity! The long and the short! The naked and the dead!"

"Um," I said. "The shoes and the socks?"

"Not quite it. Try another."

"The insipid and the juvenile," my mother said.

"The matter and the antimatter," I said.

"The whos-its and the whats-its?"

"There's this episode of *Star Trek* where they have to keep the matter and the antimatter separate because if they ever mix, do you know what happens?"

"No," he said. "What happens?"

"The whole entire universe blows up!"

"See?" he said to my mother, holding up a speared meatball with his fork. "Mix the sweet and the savory. And that's what happens."

SATURDAY. My father and mother sat on the sofa, facing the blank TV screen and talking about his return as principal at Beth Israel Congregation. It was raining and I sat on the living room floor, sorting my baseball cards. I had my whole day planned. I would sort my baseball cards until lunchtime, eat lunch, then continue sorting my baseball cards until 2:00 p.m. Then I would go into my room and finish reading an Agatha Christie mystery I had borrowed from the library, *The Murder on the Links*. I was on page 162. Reading about thirty pages an hour, I would finish by 4:00 p.m. Then I would lie on my bed and blink at the ceiling, absorbing the shock and surprise of who the killer was. I would try not to think about my first day of junior high, only two days away.

My father finished telling my mother all the things Beth Israel Congregation was making him do. They wanted to hold weekly meetings with him to "check in" and he was supposed to write progress reports every month. My mother sighed. "A small price to pay," she said, "considering you never went to see that psychiatrist."

I grabbed another handful of baseball cards from the box and kept sorting. I had 3,394 at last count, not including duplicates. Sometimes I sorted by teams, other times by position or the month the player was born. Today I was sorting by the state, country, or U.S. territory of birth. Which state would have the most? California and New York and Pennsylvania seemed to be in contention, tall burgeoning piles, while states like Rhode Island or Idaho didn't have a chance.

"They want to have another meeting on Monday," he said, matter-of-factly.

"On Labor Day?"

"What can I do? They're my employers."

"Who ever heard of a meeting on Labor Day? It's un-American."

"In point of fact, it's *quintessentially* American. 'The business of America is business.' Calvin Coolidge."

"Wonderful. Now you're quoting Calvin Coolidge."

He turned to me, his eyes gleaming.

"Did you know that Calvin Coolidge was president the year I was born?" he said. "Quick quiz. Who was president the year *you* were born? Extra-credit question. Who was vice president?"

The next card was Frank Howard, my favorite Senator, and though I knew by heart how many home runs he had hit from 1965 through 1971 (21, 18, 36, 44, 48, 44, and 26) I had never bothered to notice what state he was born in. I looked at his picture, the huge boulder head, the blond crew cut, the wire-rim glasses. Once I turned over this card, I would know where Frank Howard was born and I would know it for the rest of my life.

"Dwight Eisenhower and Richard Nixon," I said quickly, staring at the card. Frank Howard looked like he was from a state I had never been to—Montana or Texas maybe.

"Correct and correct!" my father said.

I turned over the card and looked under the line where it said whether he batted right or left handed. Born: September 17, 1932; Columbus, Ohio. I had never been to Ohio either.

My mother put down her coffee and shifted on the sofa so she could face my father directly. "What kind of meeting are they having with you?"

"Which meeting? There are lots of meetings."

"The meeting on Labor Day."

"Oh, it's nothing," he said, waving his hand. "They want to talk about instituting letter grades with pluses and minuses. *Very* important I attend this meeting."

"Good for you," my mother said. "You've been pushing letter grades for years. It's about time they listened to you."

My father stared straight ahead out the window, the rain beading up against the double panes. "I find myself, at this point in time, unalterably *opposed* to letter grades," he said.

My mother followed my father's gaze out toward the rain dripping off the willow tree in our front yard.

"Since when?"

"Since recently," he said, now looking at her. "I've had a change of heart."

"Why don't you explain that to me," she said. "Your change of heart."

"I would be delighted to explain it to you," he said. "I consider letter grades an offense against the true spirit of learning. Pluses and minuses compound the sin. Any questions?"

"I've got many questions," my mother said. "You don't want to hear them."

My father turned again to me, the cushions on the sofa squeaking. "You understand what I'm saying," he said, like I was part of the conspiracy.

"Not really," I said. I understood that in Hebrew school you got either an O for outstanding, an S for satisfactory, or a U for unsatisfactory. During my six long years attending classes, I didn't know a single kid who had ever gotten an O or a U on their report card.

"Quick quiz. Name a biblical figure and tell me what grade they would receive."

My mother rolled her eyes. She let out a little throat cluck of disgust.

"Well," I said. "Adam ate the apple and got kicked out of the Garden of Eden. So I guess Adam would get an Unsatisfactory?"

"Perhaps. But consider that he was the father of the human race. In my mind, that bumps him up to Satisfactory. Now, who would get an Outstanding?"

"God?"

My father laughed. "Yes, of course, but He's the One giving out the grades so it doesn't count. Who else?"

"Moses?" I said.

"Very good. But think about it. He disobeyed God by striking the rock instead of talking to it. He was not permitted to enter the land of Israel. Does that sound like an Outstanding to you?"

"I guess not."

My mother jumped in. "What about all those children of Israel Moses led across the desert, with all the complaining and the making of the golden calf? Under your brilliant system, do they get a Satisfactory also?"

"Well . . . ," my father said, scratching his nose, "perhaps."

"Terrific," my mother said. "So Moses gets an S, just like every other poor schmuck schlepping across the desert. Great system you've got there."

My father blinked his eyes in irritation. He continued looking at me.

"Now you understand my point?"

"I think so," I said.

"Why don't we get rid of grades altogether?" my mother said, addressing the raindrops. "How about that?"

"Why don't we just assign a number to evaluate each student, from 0 to 4.000?" he shot back. "Oh, look. I got a 3.485 in Jewish history. I got a 2.874 in conversational Hebrew. I call that empty and meaningless quantification."

"Really? I call that *grading*."

"Why don't they just assign a number to every person?"

"They do, Murray. It's called Social Security."

"*Yes*, but they don't evaluate your worth based on that number. Maybe we should all walk around with our numerical values stenciled on our foreheads. Person A is a 6.439. Person B is a 6.438. Is Person A better than Person B? Would you hire Person A over Person B? What if Person A is Hitler and Person B is Gandhi? Can we adjust the numbers? Is that allowed?"

"You're not making any sense." Now she looked worried. "Are you feeling all right?"

"Never better."

It made sense to me. Willie Mays had 636 lifetime home runs. Ed Brinkman had 63. Willie Mays was therefore ten times better than Ed Brinkman. It wasn't complicated.

"So let's talk about your Labor Day meeting," my mother said. "You're going to argue with them over letter grades and pluses and minuses? Do you think it's wise to put up a big fight? Considering?"

"I'm not going to argue," he said. "That's the genius of it all."

"Why don't you explain to me the genius of it all."

He raised his arms like he was a magician conjuring white rabbits out of the sofa cushions.

"I will say, 'You know what, Rabbi? You know what, President Harold Feinbaum? That's a *great* idea.' They will be stunned, because just last week I expressed my opposition—in writing—to letter grades with pluses and minuses. Feinbaum will say, 'You're joking, right?' I will respond, 'Why would I joke about something as important as letter grades with pluses and minuses?' I will deliver that sentence without a trace of sarcasm. Then they will say, 'When you say it's a great idea, you probably mean it's a great idea, *BUT*. What's the *BUT*? Tell us the *BUT*.' And I will respond, 'There's no *BUT*. A great idea is a great idea. You are, both of you, Rabbi and President Harold Feinbaum, brilliant and accomplished educators, and I completely trust your judgment as pertaining to the issue of letter grades with pluses and minuses.'"

He paused, looking at me. "And I will deliver *that* sentence with sincerity and honesty," he said. "And without the slightest subatomic particle of sarcasm."

But, but, but. Every time he said it, his voice got loud and scary, like a cry of pain from some wild animal caught in a trap. I looked at my baseball cards scattered in a ridiculous jumble on the floor, all those stupid piles, fifty-three of them for each state, the District of Columbia, Puerto Rico, and "Other" representing foreign countries like Cuba and the Dominican Republic. What difference did it make which state had the most cards? Who cared?

"I'm confused," my mother said calmly, like she was talking to a child. "First, you say there is an important meeting on Labor Day, and then you say it's nothing. Then you've always been in favor of letter grades, but now you say you're against them. And finally, you tell me you're going to show up at this meeting and tell them letter grades are the greatest thing since sliced bread?"

"I'm being strategic. Do you know what that means?" He glanced at me. Was he asking me too? Then he said, "Strategy is the art of getting what you want."

"And *what* do you want, Murray?" she said. I picked up the California and Ohio piles and dropped them into the box.

"What do you want?" she asked again, this time her voice quiet and sad. He went back to looking at the rain, never answering the question.

SUNDAY, IT WAS STILL RAINING. "For Pete's sake, it's a holiday weekend," my father said to us at the breakfast table. "Let's go to a movie." He crinkled the newspaper.

"Sure," my mother said. She dunked his soggy tea bag into her cup. "Why not?"

"What have we got here?" he said, looking over the movie listings. "Billy, what do you want to see?"

"I don't know."

"Here we go!" he shouted. "The dollar movie at the Flower Theatre. *Love Story.*"

"He's a twelve-year-old boy," she said. "Of course he doesn't want to see *Love Story.*"

"Why shouldn't an intelligent and sensitive boy on the cusp of adolescence see a movie about two people in love?" he said. "What's wrong with that?" I cringed at the words "intelligent," "sensitive," and "adolescence."

"It's not the kind of movie he would like."

"How do you know? Why should he only see movies with people chasing each other in snazzy convertibles? There's more to life than big explosions."

She shook her head. "All I know is: it's a movie for grown-ups." She looked at me. "It's a tragic story. It might upset him."

"Isn't life full of tragic stories?" he asked.

"Isn't there a James Bond movie playing somewhere?" she asked.

"Hah!" he shouted gleefully. "Snazzy convertibles. Big explosions. I rest my case."

"You should both go," I said. "I'll stay here." I had never been left at home alone before. They both looked at me as if I had just volunteered to launch rockets or perform surgery. Couldn't they trust a sensitive and intelligent adolescent to stay home alone for a couple of hours?

"No," my father said. "We go as a family."

"What else is playing?" my mother said.

"I'll see it," I said quietly.

"Really?" said my father.

"You don't have to see it," my mother said, frowning at me. "Stand up for yourself. Are you sure you actually want to see a movie called *Love Story*?"

"I think so," I said. "There's this really funny part—in the *Mad Magazine* satire—where Ali MacGraw is on her deathbed and the doctor says she's dying of 'old movie disease.'"

"Fantastic—old movie disease!" my father said. "See? He *wants* to see it."

My mother rolled her eyes. "*Mad Magazine*. Wonderful."

A couple of hours later, we sat in the Flower Theatre, surrounded by couples and senior citizens, waiting for *Love Story* to start. I was the only kid there. I told myself there were three good reasons for seeing this movie. First, of course, was the *Mad Magazine* satire. The rule was: the stupider the movie, the funnier the satire. The *Love Story* satire was already funny, even though I hadn't seen the actual movie. How much funnier would the satire be if—as I expected—I saw the actual movie and it turned out to be incredibly stupid?

Second, even though it wasn't rated X, I wanted to see a grown-up movie none of the other kids would see. I was going into junior high and maybe I could smoke cigarettes and brag that I had gone to see *Love Story*, and that—really—it was no big deal. A kid in my sixth-grade class had snuck into *Midnight Cowboy*, but he said it was boring and there wasn't a single naked woman in it during the half hour he was there before the theater manager kicked him out.

And finally, I suspected that my father and mother were beginning to hate each other. Maybe seeing a movie called *Love Story* would turn hate to love, like a magician turning a shiny black stick into a bouquet of flowers. Even turning hate to mild liking would be okay. It could work, in theory.

The movie started. They showed the Harvard campus and Ryan O'Neal said something about a girl who dies and how he doesn't know what to say about it. I rolled my eyes—this was going to be unbelievably stupid. But then the movie got going, and I had to admit, it wasn't that bad. Then came the big Ali MacGraw death scene. My lip quivered. *Old movie disease, old movie disease*, I chanted in my head. But I still felt like crying. I stared straight ahead, my head rock still, not wanting to watch my parents watching, not wanting them to see me watching. Sniffles percolated throughout the theater. Some guy behind us blew his nose. My father let out a sigh, like a small tire deflating. My mother was quiet. I thought about those guys who wrote the *Mad Magazine* satires. How did they do it? How could they sit through stories of heart-wrenching tragedy and death, yet feel no sadness, feel no tears in their eyes to secretly wipe away or blink back? And how could I become like them?

The movie ended. *Love means never having to say you're sorry.* My father's eyes were shiny, my mother's dry. Her face was blank, like she was marching out of the dry cleaners or the grocery store. I faked a few racking coughs so if my eyes were red or teary, they would think it was from my hay fever.

"What did you think?" my father said in a low sorrowful voice.

I coughed and sniffled. "I guess it was okay," I said.

"I didn't care for it," my mother said.

We walked to the car in silence. As soon as my father shut his car door, he said, "In my opinion, there's something wonderful and inspiring about two people from different walks of life falling in love. Romeo and Juliet. It's an old story."

"Yeah, it's an old story all right," my mother said, tight lipped. "And look how it always ends."

"How does it always end?" He pulled into traffic.

"Lots of trouble and carrying on and then somebody dies."

"Only in the movies," he said.

"We should be so lucky."

"Do you know what Ali MacGraw's last name was in the *Mad Magazine* satire?" I called up to the front seat.

"Why not look at the bright side?" my father said to my mother.

"Easy for you to say."

"Cowsnowski-Bumstein . . . Pastafoozala," I said, my voice trailing off. It was starting to rain again.

"And then there's this whole business about love meaning never having to say you're sorry," my mother said. "What *is* that?"

"Sublime," my father said, "is what it is."

"So in other words, if one person loves another, he can treat her with disrespect and hatefulness and he—that person—doesn't have to apologize?"

"That's not what it means."

"Okay, you're the big expert on true love. Tell me. What does it mean?"

He turned on the windshield wipers.

"It means when you love someone, when you bond on a spiritual level, you know each other so intimately that any offense is automatically understood. And it would be a pointless redundancy, a meaningless formality, to say 'I'm sorry.'"

"That makes no sense."

"It makes lots of sense. 'I'm sorry' is what you say when you bump into a stranger on the sidewalk."

"So you can say 'I'm sorry' to a complete stranger, but you can't say it to your wife?"

He turned off the windshield wipers. I guess it wasn't raining that hard.

"What do you think, Billy?" he asked over his shoulder.

"I don't know."

"You're the one who wanted to see this idiotic movie," my mother said.

"Well . . . ," I said. Didn't she realize I had my own problems, that I had to go to junior high in just two days? So if love meant never having to say you're sorry, then it was only logical to conclude that hate meant having to apologize constantly. Maybe that wouldn't be such a bad thing?

"I guess it kind of makes sense," I said.

"Naturally you take his side," she said. "Why do I even bother asking?"

"There are no sides in this family," my father said. "We're all one big side."

We got home. My father whispered in my ear as we walked

from the car to our front door. "Cowsnowski-Bumstein . . . Pastafoozala," he said. "Now *that's* funny."

"WHEN ARE YOU COMING BACK?" my mother asked on Monday, Labor Day, the sun shining. We sat around the breakfast table, three spokes in a wheel. My father wore his navy blue, double-breasted suit with the shiny gold buttons.

"Hard to say," he said. He seemed nervous. "There's a lot to cover."

"Of course," she said. "The letter grades with the pluses and minuses."

"It's all of a piece," he said, smoothing the sparse strands of hair across his bald head.

"What in the world does that mean?"

"It means," he said, smiling at me, "everything happens for a reason, and who are we to question it?"

"Do I have to go to Sears today?" I asked.

My father looked at his face in the shiny side of the toaster. "Nose hairs," he said. "Where are the scissors?"

"Nose hairs you're worried about?" my mother said. "For a meeting with Harold Feinbaum? The man is a fat slob."

"You're the one who's always saying I need to look more professional."

"Under the sink in the bathroom."

After my father dealt with his nose hairs, he took a deep breath and walked out the front door. My mother drove me to Sears to buy junior high clothes.

"I don't enjoy this any more than you do," she said, as we climbed out of the car in the Sears parking lot.

I doubted that very much. I doubted that there was a

human being on the planet who enjoyed anything less than I enjoyed shopping for clothes with my mother. She would point to some shirt or jacket or pair of pants, say *how about this*, and I would automatically say *I guess so* because all I wanted was to get out of there as fast as possible. I especially did not enjoy trying on pants because she would make me parade around in public and twirl, then stand still like a freak while she pulled on the waistband and asked me about the fit in the crotch.

At Sears we got on the escalator down to the Boys' Department, the dungeon. The place was mobbed with kids, mothers, fathers. A brilliant idea burst into my brain. What if the government sent you your clothes every year, just like they sent a tax form to your house? Every year, they could have some big meeting in the White House and decide on next year's clothes for seventh grade, eighth grade, ninth grade, and so on. Whatever "styles" or "fashions" they decided on at the big meeting would be fine with me. Then, they could send you your shirts, pants, underwear, and socks in whatever size your parents marked down on the tax form. All you would have to do is open a box and put on the clothes.

I wished my father was with us so I could tell him about my idea. *Interesting concept*, he would say, squinting his eyes in thought. *What else could the government take care of for you?* Dentist and doctor appointments? Haircuts? Perhaps not. Even if the government did something with medicine or hair care, you'd still have doctors and dentists and barbers prodding and poking you. There was no way around that. I looked over at my mother on the escalator. A shiny lick of hair hung down over her forehead. I guessed she wouldn't want to hear about my idea.

We stepped off the escalator and followed the Back-to-School signs, like Hansel and Gretel following a trail of poisonous bread crumbs. The first stop was tennis shoes. Government tennis shoes wouldn't work, because you had to try on different sizes to see what fit. Also, I actually cared about sneakers. I wanted to get either Chuck Taylor's because they made you look cool, or P.F. Flyers because according to the commercial, they made you run faster and jump higher. But at Sears, I only had one choice. Jeepers.

"White or black?" my mother said. We stood in front of the Jeepers bins marked SUPER SALE.

"White."

"White shows a lot of dirt. Are you sure?"

"Yes."

"Great," she said, rolling her eyes. "High-tops or low-tops?"

"Well . . ."

"Which?"

Low-tops were susceptible to "flat tires," which happened when you were walking down the hallway and somebody intentionally stepped on the back of your shoe. I knew that flat tires happened *all the time* to seventh graders in junior high. High-tops were resistant to flat tires—and they looked cooler—but they were a pain. You had to use brute force to cram your foot into the shoe, then you had to untie and loosen the laces when you took them off.

"I can't decide," I said.

"For God's sake, just pick one," she said, grabbing a pair of low-tops. People were standing behind us, waiting to get at the bin. Kids were sitting in the aisles, trying on shoes. Faraway, I could hear a baby crying its head off.

Blam! My mother threw the shoes back into the bin with a loud rattle. I looked at her and our eyes met.

"Who ever heard of a meeting on Labor Day?" she said, her eyes boring into me.

"Black low-tops," I said.

"Fine. You know what? Let's get them and go home."

"Okay." I tried on the black low-tops in size 8E and they fit on the first try. I wore them home. We found my father sitting on the couch, staring at the blank television screen.

"Your meeting's over already?"

"It's over," he said. There were tears in his eyes. "It's all over."

He sighed. It was the same way he used to sigh when he had his nervous breakdown last spring.

"Did you get fired?"

"No," he said softly. The way he said it, whatever happened was much worse.

"What then? What is it? What's all over?"

"The letter grades," he said sadly, "with the pluses and minuses."

"*What's* all over?"

He looked at her, then looked at me. "I'm sorry," he said.

Should I tell him my idea about the government sending kids back-to-school clothes? Maybe it would cheer him up.

"I got new shoes," I said, sticking out a black low-topped foot.

He went back to staring at the shiny blank television screen. *But, but, but.* It haunted me, that high desperate squeak. I knew it wasn't about the letter grades with the pluses and minuses.

· 9 ·

A Negative Times a Negative

IT WASN'T SO BAD, getting beaten up. My jaw throbbed, my lip was bleeding, and my stomach ached, but the tooth that had been tormenting me had stopped hurting. It was a miracle. I poked at it with my tongue. There was no pain, no worry that I would have to tell my mom and go to the dentist. Maybe this was how it worked. A bad thing and another bad thing make a good thing. Jaw and stomach pain cancel out tooth pain. A negative times a negative equals a positive.

I dusted myself off. Ms. Marvin had caused me all sorts of problems with the hex list. *Negative.* Then she disappeared and caused me to get beaten up. *Negative.* But now she was gone, and I wouldn't have to think about her for the rest of my life. *Positive.*

This was how inventors felt. Maybe I would write a letter to the President of the United States and the Secretary-General of the United Nations: *Dear Sirs, I have determined a secret law that controls the fate of humanity—negative times negative equals positive. Feel free to share this with all the peoples of the world....*

I WALKED INTO THE LOBBY of my building. It was 4:38 p.m. My mother would be home at 5:30. The elevator door opened and an old lady in a bathrobe got off, almost bumping into me. She stared at my bloody shirt and made a gasping noise. "My God," she said. "What happened to you?"

"Nothing," I said, sliding past her and getting on the elevator. I pressed the up button and tongued my tooth. Still no pain. My dentist didn't believe in Novocain. He gave you a wad of Kleenex to twist while he drilled deep into your tooth nerve. What if dentists punched you in the mouth to cure your toothache, instead of drilling the tooth nerve? I would take that trade. You wouldn't even have to go to a dentist because your friends or family could smack you in the mouth within the privacy and comfort of your own home.

Our apartment was cold and dark and smelled like dirty dishes. I wished I could tell my father about my toothache idea. He would laugh and tell me that four out of five dentists surveyed recommend drilling. He would tell me that my idea would most definitely not be endorsed by the American Dental Association.

In the bathroom, I looked in the mirror. I had a black eye, a dark purple bruise on my jaw, and dried blood on my face. I washed off the blood, but what could I do about the black eye and the bruises? On TV shows, people were always pressing raw steaks against their faces. We only had ground hamburger meat. Would that work?

I went to my room and changed shirts, throwing the bloody one onto the floor. My mom was always bugging me to use the laundry hamper sitting in the corner. I hardly ever did because it was too much trouble. It had a plastic lid. You couldn't throw in hook shots or jump shots from across the room. You had to actually walk up to the hamper, lift the lid, and drop in your clothes.

But my bloody shirt looked like some dead carcass lying on the floor, so I picked it up and put it in the laundry hamper. Then I gathered up all the dirty clothes on my floor and put them in the hamper too, burying the shirt.

I turned on the television and laid on my bed. My heart thumped. *Match Game 1971*. Everything was going to be fine. Negative times negative equaled positive. The first question was: "When Johnny walked into the locker room, he was worried that his BLANK wouldn't be big enough." The audience laughed. While it was most definitely true that negative times negative was positive, wasn't it also true that negative times negative *times negative* was another negative? What if some other horrible thing happened? *Dear Mr. President and Secretary-General: It has occurred to me that the secret law I discovered may have a flaw. A fatal flaw. . . .*

On *Match Game 1971*, Gene Rayburn repeated, "When Johnny walked into the locker room, he was worried that his BLANK wouldn't be big enough." The first celebrity panelist wrote "locker" on his card. The next celebrity, a woman, wrote "gym bag." What a stupid show. "Dick." "Balls." That's what I would write on my little card.

I heard the key rattling in the front door lock, heard my mother tromping in, throwing her keys down on the coffee table. "I'm home," she called out. She sounded tired.

"I'm here," I called back, over the droning laughter of *Match Game 1971*. I heard her go into the kitchen. She sighed loudly and shouted, "Billy, why didn't you put out the meat to thaw?"

"I forgot," I shouted back. This was why they had intercom systems in houses. Another bad thing about living in an apartment.

"What are we going to eat?" she said as she came into my

room. She was about to say something else, but stopped and gasped like that old lady in the bathrobe.

"Oh my God. What happened to you?"

"What do you mean?"

"What do you mean what do I mean? Have you seen your face?"

"No."

Her eyes narrowed. "Why are you wearing a different shirt?" She went for the laundry hamper and dug out my bloody shirt from the bottom of the pile.

"What happened?" She held out the shirt like it was a piece of evidence.

"I fell."

"You fell? Where?"

"I accidentally tripped over a curve."

"*Curb.*" She looked pale and wrinkly and if I squinted she kind of looked like a picture of my grandmother. "If it was an accident," she said, "why would you bury your shirt under a pile of clothes in a laundry hamper that *you never use*?"

"I don't know."

My mother turned off the TV. "Did you get into a fight?"

"Sort of."

She yanked me over to the bathroom sink and wiped my face with a wet washrag.

"Don't move," she said, leaving the bathroom. Bruises were internal injuries, but you could see them. It was Friday. I had to go to school on Monday. Everybody would ask, *what happened to you?* with those big dumb expressions on their faces. If it was summer, I could say I got hit in the face with a baseball. But now it was football season. Who gets hit in the face with a football?

My mother returned with some ice wrapped in a dish towel. She pressed it against my face. I pretended it didn't hurt.

"Tell me what happened," she said, still pressing the towel. It was cold but it burned. We were both staring at my face in the mirror.

"There were these kids I never saw before. There were three of them." I watched my mouth forming the words. My eyes stared back at me. They blinked, but I couldn't really see them blink all the way. It was impossible to see closed eyelids in a mirror. I turned away.

"Hold steady," she said. "Who were these kids?"

"I just told you," I said. "I never saw them before."

"Tell me exactly what happened."

"I was walking along North Washington Street. This car drove up and these three kids piled out and beat me up. Then they drove away."

"Did they steal anything from you?"

"No."

"Then why would they attack you for no reason?"

"Anti-Semitism, maybe. The car had Virginia license plates."

She took the cold compress from my face. "So you're just walking along the street and a bunch of anti-Semites from Virginia stop their car and attack you?"

"Pretty much."

"And you'd never seen these kids before?"

"Nope."

"So how did they know you were Jewish?"

I paused. Beads of cold water dripped down my face. "They asked me," I said. My mother clucked her tongue.

"Why would complete strangers just come up out of the blue and ask if you were Jewish?"

"How should I know?" I shrugged. "I'm not a mind reader."

She grabbed my right hand and pulled it up to the compress on my face. "Here," she said. "You hold it."

"It hurts," I said.

She talked into the mirror, arms folded. "Keep pressing. What did they say while they were attacking you?"

"Not too much," I said. "They were preoccupied with beating me up."

"I see. These boys were obviously very focused. So what did you *supposedly* say when they *supposedly* asked if you were Jewish?"

"I said, 'Yes, as a matter of fact, I am.'"

"And why would you feel compelled to give these strangers so much information? They don't need to know your business."

"Dad always said I should be proud of my Jewish heritage," I said.

"Your father said a lot of things, may he rest in peace."

"What things?" I said. Our eyes met in the mirror. She blinked and looked away. She never wanted to talk about him.

"So, to recap," she said, looking like she was grilling me in a courtroom, "you maintain you were attacked by a bunch of neo-Nazis from Virginia. Does that mean I should call the police?"

"What for?" I said. "By now they're probably over the state line."

"Good point," she said. "I'll contact the FBI."

I tongued my bad tooth. Still no pain.

She glared at me. "You're just like your father with these ridiculous stories. Now tell me what *really* happened."

"Why don't you tell me what *really* happened?" I said into the mirror, she and I watching our faces like a TV show. Her face twitched. She knew what I was talking about.

ON SUNDAY MORNING, I had another appointment with Rabbi Weinberg to discuss my Thursday bar mitzvah. This time I was meeting with him by myself. My mother drove me. She kept her eyes on the road, not speaking. She had seemed tense all weekend, more than usual. Probably—I decided—she was worried the rabbi would see the bruises on my face, decide I was a juvenile delinquent, and refuse to do my Thursday bar mitzvah. Which wouldn't necessarily be a bad thing.

She pulled into the synagogue's horseshoe-shaped driveway and stopped the car. "I'll pick you up in an hour or so. It might be longer," she said.

"Where are you going?" I said.

"Just some errands."

I opened the car door. "Let's not have any drama," she said. "Just go along with whatever the rabbi says. And don't tell him you got into a fight. He doesn't need to know our business."

"Okay." Maybe I needed to know our business.

"Billy?" she said softly, as I started to close the car door.

"What?"

"I love you."

Why did she have to say *that*? She never said stuff like that out loud, and it was one of the few things I admired her for. People didn't need to be walking around all day telling each other *I love you I love you*. Who needs to hear that?

The door to Rabbi Weinberg's office was closed. Through the dark mottled glass, I could make out a shadowy blob hunched over a desk. He was probably doing something important like praying or reading the Torah. Should I knock? Should I clear my throat loudly? Or should I wait until he emerged? I knocked softly, so gently even I could barely hear it. I waited a long minute. I knocked again, louder.

"Come IN," I heard, his voice booming. I opened the door. He was behind his desk, peeling an orange. He looked at me, smiling. "Hello there!"

"Billy Blumberg?" I said, in case he didn't remember me. "I have an appointment about my Thursday bar mitzvah?"

"I know," he said, motioning me to a chair. His smile sagged, a flicker of alarm. "Goodness! What happened to you?"

"Tackle football." I sat in a leather armchair facing his desk. I leaned forward.

He chuckled. "I should see the other guy, right?"

"Yeah," I said. "I guess."

"Orange?" he said, offering me a slice.

"No thank you."

He put the orange on a napkin and squinted a thoughtful expression on his face, like he was about to give a sermon.

"So. Do you play in a football league, Billy?"

"No. Just with some friends after school." What a lie. I had no friends. Could he tell?

"Terrific. What position do you play?"

"Um, there's no positions. We just go out for passes and stuff."

"Sounds like fun. So we have tackle football. What else do you like to do? Aside from studying Hebrew and Jewish history, of course."

I paused. Should I lie about that too?

"Joking!" he said, grinning. "What else do you like to do?"

"Well, I don't know. Watch TV, I guess."

"What's your favorite TV show of all time?"

"Probably . . . I would have to say . . . *Get Smart.*"

"Fantastic!" he practically shouted. "I always liked the Cone of Silence. Remember that? How did it work?"

"Well, this big glass bubble lowered down from the ceiling, and not only could nobody outside hear them talking, but they couldn't even hear each other."

"That's right!" he said, laughing. "You know, that might make a good sermon. Let me write that down. *The Cone of Silence: How Do We Talk to God?*" he said, writing on a notepad. "What do you think of that?"

"It's pretty good."

He looked at me, suddenly serious. "Now, let's talk about this Thursday bar mitzvah. You're obviously a smart young man. I know that. You know that. It's pretty minimal what you have to do on a Thursday." He stared at me, his eyes not blinking. "I know your mother wants a Thursday. Would you rather have a Saturday? I could talk to her."

"Thursday's fine," I said. "I don't care."

"You don't care?"

"I mean, I don't mind."

He picked up the orange. Then he put it down.

"I talked to the rabbi at Beth Israel. He told me about your father."

I looked over his shoulder at a plaque hanging on the wall, commemorating the planting of trees in Israel.

"He sounded like a wonderful man."

"I guess."

"You guess? You don't know?"

"Okay," I said. "I know."

"Such a tragedy—your father and then the Feinbaums. It's tempting to ask why God would let something like this happen. Whether things like this happen for a reason."

"Uh-huh."

"What do you think?"

"About what?"

"What I just said. Do you think bad things happen for a reason?"

I paused. What was I supposed to say? Weren't rabbis supposed to believe that God was everywhere and controlled everything?

"I believe that everything happens for a reason," I said.

"*Everything*? Wow." He dug into his pocket and pulled out a coin. He flipped it up in the air with one hand and caught it with the other.

"Heads! Did this nickel come up heads for a reason?"

"Well, I guess it depends on whether you called heads or not."

"Fair enough," he nodded. "So let me ask you a question. What is the reason for the tragedies that have befallen you?"

"I don't know."

"Do you think the reasons—whatever they are—have anything to do with you?"

"Maybe," I said, "but I don't really know for sure."

"What if it has *nothing* to do with you? What if bad things just happen to good people?"

"So if bad things just happen to good people, then I guess there's nothing I can do about it."

"Is that so?" he said. "I think there's always something worth doing."

"Like what?" I asked.

"Think back to the High Holidays. Righteousness, repentance, charity. How do you ensure that you're inscribed in the Book of Life?"

"Atone for my sins?"

"Yes, but how do you do that?"

"Apologize to God?"

"What else?"

What else? That seemed like plenty.

"You have to apologize to the people you've wronged," he said. "It's not enough just to tell God you're sorry. You have to tell those people and they have to grant you forgiveness. Remember, we have the power to avert the severe decree."

"What if it doesn't work?" I said, wondering if I should mention my discovery about negative times negative equaling positive.

"What if it does?" he said.

I STOOD IN THE LOBBY waiting for our dirty-white Dodge Dart. The rabbi had told me I was "on course" for my Thursday bar mitzvah. He compared me to a Boeing 747, wheels down, coming in for the smoothest of landings. Then he told me about his trip on the supersonic Concord SST. I wanted to ask if he could hear the plane breaking the sound barrier, whether it was true that all the people inside the plane had themselves broken the sound barrier, and whether it was true that when people on the plane talked to each other, that sound was going faster than any sound on the face of the earth. Instead I asked what kind of refreshments they served.

I looked through the glass door, out toward the street. A gleaming white Dodge Dart with a racing stripe drove by. What kind of person puts a racing stripe on a Dodge Dart? Maybe if I had told my mom the anti-Semitic car from Virginia had a racing stripe, she would have believed me. I grabbed a flyer from a stack next to the doorway. The flyer advertised a Coffeehouse Conclave next Saturday night, sponsored by the United Synagogue Youth—USY. The topic was "The Plight of Soviet

Jewry" and it featured a slide show by Rabbi Weinberg on his trip to Moscow and Leningrad. Was God involved in the plight of Soviet Jewry? When the rabbi flipped the coin and said that God—the President of the spirit world—wouldn't bother to make it come up heads or tails, did that mean He interfered with some things and ignored other things? Was there a selection process? Coin flip: no? People dying: yes? How about everything in between?

Another Dodge Dart, this one a light blue, drove up, slowed down, then kept going. Why did we have to have a Dodge Dart? Only *six months* after my father bought it, the car's electrical system short-circuited. He was stranded at work and had to take a taxi home. All the Dodge Darts in the world, he said, and you'd think they'd sooner or later get it right. Had God intervened in the fate of our Dodge Dart? There were millions of them, all built in the same factory, manufactured by an identical assembly line, and my father had to buy the single worst Dodge Dart ever made.

Still no dirty-white Dodge Dart. It was now an hour and a half since my mother had dropped me off. What was taking her so long?

The rabbi had told me that bad things happen to good people, but what made him think I was a good person? I was a person who had made a hex list with the names of two people who had *actually died.* Maybe I qualified as a good person if everyone on the list was bad, because negative times negative equaled positive, and doing bad to a bad person might make you a good person. But none of the people on my list were all that bad except for Bob Short—the guy who moved the Senators to Texas. On the other hand, I wouldn't consider any of the others all that great either: Harold and Lawrence Feinbaum,

Team Belgium, Brooks Robinson, Mr. Pappas . . . my mother. My mother. Where was she?

The rabbi said something about apologizing to everybody if I wanted to be inscribed in the Book of Life. Maybe that would remove the curses on my hex list. I could apologize in person to Team Belgium and to Mr. Pappas, but what about Brooks Robinson? I pulled a pencil out of my pocket and sat on the floor. I turned over the USY flyer and wrote a rough draft.

Dear Mr. Brooks Robinson,

You probably don't know this, but I put you on a hex list and you are cursed. I'm sorry. It was completely my fault and you didn't deserve it when you sprained your ankle on that patio in Florida. Actually, you've been lucky so far, because much worse things have happened to other people on the hex list. You definitely don't deserve any other horrible catastrophe that might befall you. I hope you will accept my apology.

Sincerely,
Billy Blumberg

P.S. If you accept my apology, the curse will be removed. DO YOU ACCEPT MY APOLOGY??? (check one)

Yes ___
No ___
Maybe ___
Signature ________________
Date ___________

This form was brilliant. I was a genius. Maybe I could draw one up for each person on my list. They could sign it in the comfort and privacy of their own homes. I read through the form again. Should I cross out the *Maybe* box? If they checked *Maybe* that wouldn't accomplish anything. It had to be *Yes* or *No*, black or white, negative or positive. But on the other hand . . . *maybe* . . . I had gotten the whole thing backwards. Those people were on the hex list because they had wronged me and that's why they were cursed. So maybe the way for them to avert the severe decree was for them to apologize to me. How could I know for sure? I couldn't. Maybe that was the answer: everybody had to apologize to everybody.

I heard a horn, three quick beeps. I looked up and there it was, the white Dodge Dart. I climbed in.

"Didn't you see me waiting here for you?" my mother said. She sounded strange, like she couldn't decide whether to be mad at me or not.

"Where were you?" I asked.

"I told you. Errands."

"What errands?"

"I'd appreciate not getting the third degree in my own automobile," she said, shaking her head, eyes straight ahead on the road. "How did things go with the rabbi?"

"Fine," I said. "He said you should call him. He wants to talk to you."

"About what?"

"How should I know?"

"Tell me exactly what he said."

"He said, 'Tell your mother to call me, I want to talk to her.'"

"Fine."

We drove down Veirs Mill Road, back to our apartment building. Houses, lawns, driveways zipped by, like they were on a treadmill. How would we ever apologize to each other? We were in the Cone of Silence. She said she "loved me" and it looked like Ryan O'Neal and my father were right. Love did mean never having to say you're sorry.

On the elevator up to our apartment, I realized I had left my combination USY flyer/Brooks Robinson apology form in the car. How would I ever explain it to her? I had to get it back. She had the car keys. She would want to know—exactly—what it was I left behind in the car. She always wanted to know my business. I could tell her the rabbi had given me a mimeograph sheet on preparing for a Thursday bar mitzvah. The positive was that this was believable. The negative was that she might want to see it. *Or* I could just say it was a flyer for the Saturday-night USY Coffeehouse Conclave thing. The positive: this was actually true, as long as she didn't see the other side of the flyer. The negative: she might force me to go.

I waited until the elevator got to our floor. As the doors opened, I said, "Um, I left something in the car. Can I go back and get it?"

"Yes," she said, almost a whisper. Her eyes were shiny. She gave me the car keys and headed down the long carpeted hallway.

I went back to the garage and opened the car door. There it was, folded up on the seat. But there was something else too—a business card, face down on the edge of the driver's seat. I picked it up, turned it over. It said, *Capitol Radiology, 5454 Wisconsin Avenue, Chevy Chase, Maryland.*

My tooth again started to hurt, worse than ever.

. *10* .

Impending Doom

Radiology. I imagined radioactivity and atomic bombs. That's what caused Godzilla to be transformed from a tiny lizard that might lick your ear and scamper down the back of your shirt, into a giant dragon that breathed fire and stomped buildings like upside-down paper cups. On the other hand, I remembered an episode of *Gilligan's Island* where radioactive seeds grew overnight into giant carrots and cucumbers. Therefore, wouldn't radiology be a good thing because it could end world hunger?

My mother had a dictionary on her bookshelf, but it was risky looking up *radiology* that afternoon or night. What if she saw me and wanted to know what word I was looking up and why? *Zyzzyva*, I could say. "I've always been curious about the final word in the dictionary." The problem with that was if she saw me looking up *radiology* and I told her it was *zyzzyva*, she'd see I wasn't at the end of the book. Maybe I could tell her I was looking up *rutabaga*. "You probably don't know this about me," I could say, "but I've always been fascinated by interesting vegetables."

The more lies I told, the worse I got at it. How could that be? If I was a criminal and cracked safes or picked pockets, wouldn't I keep getting better? My lying should be like riding a bike, but for me it was the opposite. At first I was smooth and confident, zipping around tricky corners at top speed. Now I was shaky and jittery, almost falling onto hard pavement, almost scraping the sides of parked cars, my hands sweaty and white-knuckled on the handlebars. Every time I lied to someone, I felt impending doom, as if the worst thing in the world was going to happen to me and that one day I would be forced to tell the truth about everything.

On Monday morning, I got to school early and headed straight for the school library.

The library was cool, quiet, and empty. Tucked off in the corner was a huge Webster's dictionary on a wooden stand, like a tree stump in a forest. The pages were splayed open at the *j*'s. What word had been looked up? *judgment, juggernaut, jugular.* I checked my watch—only five minutes until homeroom started. I flipped the pages, thick handfuls at a time until I got to the *r*'s, *ra*'s, *rad*'s:

radiology *noun:* The branch of medicine that deals with the use of radioactive substances in diagnosis and treatment of disease.

My heart raced, my jugular vein pounded. So this meant my mother had a disease? It must be serious. She acted tired and unhappy all the time. And it wasn't just after my father died. She was tired and unhappy before that too. But on the other hand, she never stayed home from work, so how sick could she be? If I had a disease that had something to do with radioactivity, I would stay home from school as many weeks as possible, eating breakfast and lunch in bed, watching TV game shows.

The bell rang for homeroom. I had two minutes. I flipped the pages backward to the *m*'s—covering my tracks—and hurried out. What would I do if something happened to my mother? Who would take care of me?

As I walked into homeroom, everybody stopped talking, looked at me, and started whispering. It was written on my face: *my mother is getting radiology and she has a serious disease and I may have to live in an orphanage.* Then I remembered. It wasn't my mother. It was the hex list. A negative times a negative. At the exact same moment I'm worrying about radiology, the hex list problem smacks me across the face. From what direction would the positive come? It was hard to imagine.

I sat down. Hushed silence, like when a judge enters a courtroom. Then, the kid to my right—red hair, his last name starting with an A or a B, just like everybody in my homeroom—started talking in a loud voice to the kid in front of him.

"Did you hear about Pappas?" he said.

"No!" said the other kid, in a fake way, as if he had already heard all about it.

Red hair said that Mr. Pappas's finger, the one he banged against the blackboard, had gotten infected, that the infection had spread into his forehead, that on Saturday night he was yelling at his wife and "all of a sudden" a blood vessel in his forehead popped and he had a stroke. He spent all day Sunday in his bedroom drooling and watching soap operas and game shows on TV. A team of doctors examined him and declared him a certifiable vegetable.

"Poor Pappas," said the other kid, shaking his head. Neither of them looked at me, but I could tell they were *forcing* themselves not to look at me. I knew there were no game shows or soap operas on Sunday TV, and that—therefore—this story must be a lie. But I didn't say anything.

After homeroom, I walked to first period. Was everyone in the hallway—even the ninth graders—looking at me or was it my imagination? I passed by Mrs. Dobson, the pretty typing teacher who looked like Barbara Eden. Even *she* looked at me. Her face twitched, then she looked away. Why would her face twitch? Maybe she had a nervous condition. Maybe I reminded her of someone from long ago, a boy she knew in junior high who had broken her heart. Maybe she had a toothache.

Then I remembered the bruise on my face. That's why everybody was looking! People loved to see blood, even if it was below the skin. But on the other hand, why would ninth graders care about some stupid little seventh grader with a bruised face? Ninth graders had more important things to worry about, like stabbing people and breaking into cars. I passed by the teachers' lounge. What were Mrs. Dobson and all the other teachers saying about me in that room?

I wished I had a secret friend. Someone I could trust, someone who actually liked me. My friend would tell me if everybody was talking about me, and if so, what they were saying. He might hold a few things back because he wouldn't want to hurt my feelings, but I'd say no, tell me everything. We would work out a system. He would leave notes in my locker. Like, for example: *9:52 a.m.: outside Room 232, hallway on right side heading north, overheard unidentified female eighth grader say, and I quote: "he's really creepy and funny looking." I'm pretty sure she was talking about you.*

FIRST PERIOD, social studies. The substitute wrote his name on the board: *Mr. Dannemeyer.* He turned to the class and said, "Mr. Pappas is ill. He will be out for the rest of the week."

"What's wrong with him?" asked Kurt Johnson. He just blurted it out, not even raising his hand.

"Bronchitis," the sub said. "That's all I know about it."

About *it*. So, in other words, there was some situation, an *it* that was so horrible they wouldn't even tell a substitute teacher the true story.

Then Kurt said—in a totally not sarcastic way—"Is Mr. Pappas going to be okay?"

Since when did a guy like Kurt Johnson care about the health and welfare of a teacher? My face felt hot, as if the bruise on my face had started to glow.

"I'm sure he'll be fine," said the sub.

How the hell did he know? If he was a doctor, he wouldn't be a substitute teacher. On the other hand, maybe he flunked out of medical school, but before flunking out he had already taken the class on bronchitis or strokes or whatever really happened to Mr. Pappas, so he knew what he was talking about.

I wondered if Mr. Dannemeyer knew anything about radiology. Was my mother going to be all right? Why did I have to put her on my hex list? If I had to go to an orphanage, would it be in the Washington metropolitan area, or do they ship you to Oklahoma or Iowa or wherever they have a vacancy?

Usually with a substitute teacher, everybody laughs and talks and throws things. But this time, the class was hushed. I looked over at Danielson, and he wasn't drawing. He just sat there, his black Flair pen capped, staring at a blank piece of paper.

The lights went off and we spent the rest of the period watching a long boring movie about New Zealand. The room's cool darkness and the smooth clicking of the projector relaxed me. I told myself that whenever I have a hunch about something, a deep-down feeling that something horrible has to be true, I'm always *always* wrong. There was the time in sixth grade I went through a string of inexplicable mishaps. During a three-day period, I tripped over an elevated sidewalk crack, dropped a glass of grape juice onto the kitchen floor, accidentally stabbed myself in the hand with a sharp pencil, and mysteriously lost the ability to judge fly balls in the outfield. I suspected—no, I *knew*—I had Lou Gehrig's disease. But I was wrong and I was fine. Therefore, I must be wrong about my mother and the hex list and everything else. I must have nothing to worry about.

I looked around the room. Everyone stared at the screen, like they were being hypnotized. Everyone except for Kurt. He was looking at me, his face blank, like *he* was being hypnotized. I looked back at the screen. The movie showed a flock of sheep dotting the side of a big hill. The narrator said that there were more sheep in New Zealand than people. If sheep could become intelligent, like the monkeys in *Planet of the Apes*, would they take over New Zealand? On the one hand, there would be lots more of them, and they have teeth and sharp hooves. But on the other hand, sheep don't have arms and opposable thumbs, so how would they hold knives and guns if there was a revolution? In their teeth maybe. Then maybe the peoples of the world would come to the aid of their fellow humans in New Zealand. But then again, why bother? If the president of New Zealand was a sheep, would that be so bad?

The bell rang before the movie ended. The lights clicked on and the movie projector clicked off. "We'll watch the rest of it tomorrow," said the substitute. I hurried into the hallway, head down, avoiding eye contact. I felt someone grab my arm.

"Come here for a second," Kurt said, his eyes blinking. He pulled me into an empty doorway. He stared at me. "Did your father really kill himself?" he said.

"Yes." Had he forgotten that he had beaten me up? It was like it had never happened.

Then he said, "My grandfather had a heart attack over the weekend."

"Oh," I said. "Sorry."

He stared at me.

"Do you think that has to do with the curse?"

"I don't know."

He stared at me some more.

"Probably," I said.

"You have to remove my curse!"

"I don't know how," I said. "You saw it. Ms. Marvin—Nancy—doesn't live there anymore. Remember? That was right before you beat me up."

"You have to do something!" He grabbed my arm again.

"I'll think of something," I said. "Meet me at lunch period."

"No," he said. "You have to do something *now*."

"Okay, there's one other thing that might work."

"Do it." He tightened his grip on my arm.

There was only a minute until second period. I talked fast. "We have to apologize to each other. First me. I'm sorry I put you on the hex list. Now tell me you accept my apology."

"What?"

"Say, 'I accept your apology.'"

"I accept your apology."

"Okay. Now you."

"Now me what?" Kurt said.

"Say you apologize to me."

"What for?"

"For beating me up, for starters."

"Right. Sorry about that."

"And also for not doing any work on Team Belgium."

"How do you know this is gonna work?" He looked skeptical.

The halls were emptying. It was almost time for second period.

"I met with this rabbi and he said that's what I have to do. It has to do with the Book of Life and averting the severe decree . . ."

"*What?*"

". . . and things like that. It's very complicated. Come on, hurry! Say it!"

"I apologize for beating you up and for not doing any work on Team Belgium."

"I accept your apology," I said. "The curse is hereby officially removed."

"Are you sure?"

Of course I wasn't sure. I wasn't sure about anything.

"Yes," I said, "I'm sure."

He released my arm. I had to ask. Maybe Kurt would be my secret friend. "Everybody's acting really weird today," I said. "Is something going on?"

"What do you think?" Kurt said, like he was annoyed I was stupid enough to even ask.

IN THE MIDDLE OF MY MATH CLASS, the vice principal of West Montgomery Junior High, Mr. Dixon, walked into the classroom. "Excuse me, Mr. Schultz," he said. Our algebra teacher, Mr. Schultz, stopped writing on the blackboard:

$3x + 4y = 21$

If $y = 6$

$x = ?$

This *never* happened. Vice principals never interrupted a class. He wasn't coming in to wish us a nice day and congratulate us on working hard. Either a person in someone's family had died, or somebody was in so much trouble they had actually thought about calling the police. Mr. Dixon was bald—a death's head with horn-rimmed glasses and a black formal suit. His eyes scanned up and down the rows, searching our faces. How would he even know what I looked like? Did he have all our pictures in some file, like wanted posters in the post office?

"Mr. Blumberg?" he said, his eyes locking in on me. "Come with me, please."

Heads swiveled, chairs squeaked. Everyone gaped at me like I was a dead body swinging at the end of a rope. Mr. Dixon looked solemn. Light glinted off his bald head. He raised his right arm toward me, one finger extended. I gathered my books and walked out with him, feeling his hand on the small of my back. I was going to be expelled. I would never find out what x equaled if $y = 6$.

We marched down the hallway, not talking, eyes straight ahead. He smelled like aftershave and his leather shoes squeaked against the floor. We went into the main office, and even the secretary at the front desk looked away. Mr. Dixon headed into a back room behind the front desk. I stopped. Was I supposed to follow him?

"Don't stop now," he said, turning back to me with an expression of mock surprise. "You're almost there."

I followed him into his office.

"Shut the door and sit down, Mr. Blumberg."

I shut the door and sat in a metal chair facing his desk. The desk was almost bare: just a plant, a phone, a pencil holder, a lamp, a ticking clock, and a bright smooth manila folder arranged perfectly in front of his chair.

Mr. Dixon stared across the desk at me. One second, five seconds, ten seconds. His eyes bored into me, his eyebeams concentrated and magnified by his thick glasses. Was I supposed to say something? I looked at the rest of his face, the lines on his forehead, the pimple on his nose, the mouth not smiling or frowning, just a flat line like a distant horizon at the edge of a barren wasteland. I looked at the plant in a clay pot on the far corner of the desk. It was a mini-cactus, its prickly arms reaching to the fluorescent light overhead. I looked back at Mr. Dixon and he was still staring at me. This was his technique. I knew all about techniques.

"How did you get those bruises on your face?" he said, finally, like it was my fault.

"I tripped."

"I've been a vice principal long enough to know that's not a true statement," he said. "But we'll deal with that later. Do you know why you're here?"

"Not really."

"Oh, I think that you do," he said. Then he stared at me some more. Silence, as a tool, a scalpel he could use to cut away my skin, flesh, bones. I stared back, making my face a mask, every facial muscle relaxed. Behind his glasses were a skull and a brain, just like mine.

Finally he said, "This is very disappointing. If you are totally honest with me, things are going to go a lot better for you."

More silence. I could hear him breathing.

"So," he said. "Is there anything you have to tell me?"

"No," I said. "No, sir."

He shifted in his chair, put his right hand on the edge of the manila folder.

"The fighting is one thing. Fighting is unacceptable, and we don't tolerate it in this school. But this other matter—and you know very well what I am talking about—is much worse. On a scale of one to ten, fighting is a nine. But for what you've done, we'd have to use a logarithmic scale. Not that you would know what that is."

"I do, actually," I said. "Logarithms are like using a scale of ten to one hundred, or one hundred to one thousand."

"*Very* good!" His bushy eyebrows shot up and he smiled for the first time. "So we understand each other?"

"I think so."

"*Now* do you have something to tell me?"

"Not really."

He sighed and shook his head, like he was watching a sad movie with lots of tragedy and tears and thinking to himself: such a shame, if only it didn't have to be this way.

"I was looking at your record," he said, opening the manila folder, then closing it again. "You've gotten a lot of A's throughout your academic career. You're a smart kid. Do *you* think you're a smart kid?"

"I guess so."

"Mr. Blumberg, have you ever heard of Dante's nine circles of hell?"

"No." Was this a trick question?

"Well, allow me to explain it to you. There are nine circles of hell. The lower you go, the worse it gets, and once you descend from one circle to the next circle, you can never go back. Are you with me so far?"

"I think so."

"Excellent. You are now in the first circle. You are about to descend into the second circle, where the sins of the sinner are greater and the punishments inflicted by the punisher are more horrible. You can voluntarily tell me everything right now, and you will remain in the first circle. But if you refuse to tell me everything, you will walk through that door into the second circle. Do you understand?"

"Yes." I understood what he was saying, but my sins were my sins and until I committed more of them, how would going into the new circle make them any better or any worse?

"You are now entering the second circle," he said. "The door behind you is beginning to close. Once that door closes, it is closed forever and you can't go back. Now. Is there anything you want to tell me?"

"No, sir."

"The door . . . is now closed. You are in the second circle of hell. The third circle beckons."

He again opened the manila folder, glanced at it, then closed it. "And your own father, a vice principal," he said.

"Actually, a principal," I said, "but in Hebrew school, not regular school."

"Yes," he said, "I know all about that." Knew all about what? Why was he talking about my father like he was still alive? Wouldn't the manila folder tell him that my father had killed himself? Surely the words would be in letters a lot bigger than all those A's he found in my academic record. Mr. Dixon frowned and bit his lip, as if to say he knew something important that he wished he could tell me, but the time wasn't right.

Then he stood up and said, "I will be right back. Don't even think about moving, son."

He walked out, his leather shoes squeaking. *Son.* I looked

at the reflection of the overhead fluorescent light on his shiny bare desk. Mr. Dixon was so strange. Was something going on? The logarithms, the nine circles of hell. If he knew my father was a principal, why did he say he was a vice principal? Maybe it was some secret code. Something was going on and things were not as they appeared on the surface. Maybe Mr. Dixon was my secret friend. What if he had actually *known* my father. What if they had met at a conference mixing principals and vice principals from all walks of life. And in real life, Mr. Dixon was a super nice guy, and he and my father became good friends. On the last night of the conference they might have stayed up late together, looking at constellations and talking about logarithms and the nine circles of hell. Right after they identified Orion's Belt my father said, *If anything ever happens to me, would you look after my son?* And Mr. Dixon said, *I shall, but I will be his secret benefactor and when the time is right, I will reveal myself to him.* So now, maybe he was testing me. If I resisted telling him about the curse that my father had put on my enemies . . . and if I resisted down to the ninth circle of hell, then and only then, would he . . . what?

Mr. Dixon returned, drinking coffee out of a Styrofoam cup. He sat and pushed the closed manila folder over to the side.

"Okay, let's stop fooling around here," he said. "We know you've been putting curses on students and threatening people."

"I haven't threatened anybody."

"So you *have* been putting curses on people?"

"Not really," I said.

"Not *really*? What does that mean? Have you put curses on people? Is the answer yes or no?"

"No, I haven't intentionally put a direct curse on anybody."

"What is a *direct* curse?"

"Um," I said. "A curse that someone puts on . . . directly."

"Are there other kinds of curses?"

"I guess so."

"You guess so? What are some other kinds?"

"Um . . . indirect and unintentional."

"Are *those* the kinds of curses you put on students in my school?"

"No."

"No? Then why did you tell me you didn't intentionally put a direct curse on anyone? Why didn't you just say, 'No, I never put a curse of any kind on anyone.'"

"I don't know."

"You don't know what?"

"I don't know why I said what I said."

Shaking his head, he opened the manila folder and took out a piece of notebook paper. He pushed it across the desk at me. It was the note I had written to Julie Baines, the one that hadn't been lost in the locker crevice:

Dear Julie,

Please don't tell anyone about the hex list—the one that I showed you because you wanted me to show it to you. I know you promised you wouldn't and that means you probably won't. But I thought you should know that there's a rule about how anyone who breaks a promise involving a hex list will themselves be cursed with a hex. I wish that wasn't the rule, but that's just the way that particular rule happens to be. I'm sorry. I hope you haven't broken your promise by the time you read this note.

Yours truly,
Billy Blumberg

"Did you write this?" Mr. Dixon said, taking the note back.

I said nothing. I tried to use silence as a tool.

"Did you write this?" he said again. "Your name's on it."

"Yes," I said. "I guess I did."

"So you *did* write this note. And you *have* been putting names on a hex list and putting curses on people and threatening students."

"Well . . . ," I said.

"Well what? It says it right here! Your own handwriting!"

"It was kind of a joke."

"Really? It doesn't seem funny to me. The student whose locker you put this in didn't think it was funny."

"People have different senses of humor," I said.

"Oh, really? Do *you* think this is funny?"

"No."

"I'll bet your father wouldn't have found this funny either, Mr. Blumberg."

I was now in the ninth circle. Mr. Dixon was never my secret friend. He had not met my father at a conference of principals and vice principals from all walks of life. They didn't together gaze into the starry sky. He would reveal nothing to me.

"I confess," I said. "I did it."

"Where is the list of names?"

"I threw it away."

"Isn't it true that you keep this list in a candy box with your baseball cards? Isn't that correct?" Julie Baines had told him everything. There was almost nothing left to lie about.

"Yes," I said.

"Who else is involved?"

"Nobody. I don't have any friends," I said, trying to make a negative into a positive.

"So nobody was in league with you? Nobody helped you?"

"Not really."

Mr. Dixon chuckled. "Again with the 'not really.' So somebody helped you. Who was it?"

"Some lady."

"What lady?"

"Some lady I met at the 7-Eleven."

"What's her name?"

"I don't know."

"So . . . some woman *completely unknown to you* at a 7-Eleven was in on this? You expect me to believe that?"

"No."

"I'll repeat the question. What's her name?"

"She didn't tell me."

Mr. Dixon leaned forward, his eyes boring into me. "What's her name?"

"I don't know."

Mr. Dixon wrote something on a notepad. "We're done here. For now. By the way," he said, "we've already contacted your mother. She's on her way. We'll all have a little chat."

"DON'T BREATHE A WORD until we get in the car," my mother said afterwards, her high heels clicking on the school parking lot. Her face was stretched and pale, either from radiology or from fury. I felt bad for her. She had stood up for me, refusing to show them the hex list.

"That's very unfortunate," Mr. Dixon had said. "It saddens me."

"It *saddens* you?" she had said. "You persecute an orphan whose father has recently passed away and then you pull me out of work in the middle of the day and that *saddens* you? How do you think I feel?"

Then she said the "very idea" of a hex was silly superstitious nonsense and that maybe it was the fault of the teachers and administration that the school was—to use Mr. Dixon's words—"in a panic."

"What do you people teach here?" she asked Mr. Dixon. "Astrology? Voodoo?"

"Billy told me that some woman at the 7-Eleven helped him draw up the hex list. Do you know who that might be?"

"Of course not," she said, glancing at me. "Billy likes to make things up. You know children and their active imaginations."

"What I know is that this situation is very serious," Mr. Dixon said, and he started talking about conduct rules and various punishments. He kept repeating the phrase *very serious* throughout the conversation. He was a lot nicer to her than he had been to me, and there was no mention of the nine circles of hell. But in the end, I was still suspended for a week and it was "to be determined" if I would be expelled and forced to go to reform school.

My mother and I climbed into the car. We pulled the doors shut.

She reached into her purse, pulled out my hex list, and pushed it onto my lap. *My stupid mother*, it said, in my own handwriting.

"Do you really hate me this much?"

"I'm sorry," I said. She wouldn't look at me.

She started the car. She paused, then turned off the engine. My mother rested her head on the steering wheel and started to cry. Not regular crying, but loud gasping sobs. Her whole body shook. I had only heard her cry like that one time before.

I didn't know what to do. On TV or in the movies, when

someone is crying the other person says "there, there" and pats them on the head and says everything will be okay. But how was I supposed to know if everything *would* be okay?

She looked at me. The tears were making her mascara run. "You probably deserve to know. Your father took sleeping pills."

Now I felt like crying. "I'm sorry," I said again.

"I'm sorry too. We never should have moved to Rockville."

"It's okay," I said. There, there.

. 11 .
Graphology

THE LAST TIME I saw my father alive was at breakfast on the morning of that day. We didn't have much of a conversation. He was eating his dry cereal, I was eating oatmeal. He didn't seem sad and he didn't seem happy. I was late for school, hurrying. He was still in his sky blue pajamas.

"So how are you this morning?" he asked me. I should have asked him that very same question. What would he have said?

"Fine." I ate one more spoonful of oatmeal and leapt up, grabbing my books.

"What else?" He stared into his cereal bowl. "What's going on at school today?"

"Nothing."

"That was a stupid question," he said, letting out a little sigh. "I apologize for asking it."

I stood up.

"And what I mean by that," he said, raising his face to the light overhead, squinting at me, "is that I already know what's going on at school today and every day. I used to be an education professional. I know all that. Therefore, it's a question to which I already know the answer in advance. So why am I wasting your time?"

"It's not like I care," I said, grabbing my books and rushing out.

DAY ONE OF MY SUSPENSION. I lie in bed listening to my mother rustling through the closet hangers, the clinking of breakfast dishes, faucets on and faucets off, and finally the front door closing, the key clicking the lock shut, and the vast silence of our apartment. She had barely spoken to me at dinner the night before. I had thought she'd be asking me a million questions. Didn't she have suspicions?

"I'm sorry I put your name on the hex list," I said for the millionth time, and she just replied in a voice like cold dripping water: *not now*.

If not now, when, and more importantly, what? I knew she was going to punish me and I wished she would tell me what the punishment was so I could prepare myself. She could take away privileges, except I couldn't think of any privileges I had to be taken away except for the television in my room. On the other hand, I had already been punished at school and wasn't there something in the Constitution called "double jeopardy" that prohibited American citizens from being punished twice for the same crime?

Being suspended from junior high wasn't too bad as long as I could watch TV. For most of the day, I could watch game shows—*Jeopardy*, *The Who, What, or Where Game*, *Password*, *Concentration*, *Match Game 1971*. But between 3:00 and 4:30 it was only soap operas. I called it The Zero Hour even though it lasted for ninety minutes.

My mother told me I was under "house arrest" and I wasn't allowed to leave the apartment for any reason except a fire, an explosion, or a natural disaster. I promised I wouldn't, and even if I wanted to, where was I supposed to go? I ate a handful of Cheerios straight from the box and got down to business. TV on, blinds drawn, I let it wash over me, that soothing bath of laughter and applause, the little bells ringing and buzzers buzzing, lots of blinking numbers and dancing dollar signs. Several hours went by, and then it was the Zero Hour, 3:00.

General Hospital. There was nothing to do but watch. At first I felt lost, all these people I didn't know kissing each other, yelling at each other, slapping, crying, slamming doors, storming out of rooms. It was hard to figure out what the problem was. Then I started to get it. There were two guys who had been switched at birth and now they were meeting each other for the first time in twenty-five years because they were both supposed to marry the same woman. I had two thoughts. First, there was absolutely no mention of hospitals, doctors, or illnesses. Everything took place in somebody's living room or bedroom, plus there was a scene in a bar. Why was the show called *General Hospital*? Second, the situation with the two guys and the woman got me thinking about Michael Strohman from my old school in Silver Spring, and how he and I were interested in the same girl, Pam Lowenstein. That was only two months ago, but it seemed like twenty-five years.

At 3:30 it was *One Life to Live.* Some guy had an evil twin and both of them had moustaches. What if the good twin shaved off his moustache? Problem solved! I thought some more: Michael Strohman was on my hex list and I wondered whether the curse had gotten him, just like it might have caused the Feinbaums to be killed in the car accident or Mr. Pappas to have a stroke. Maybe Michael Strohman had smoked pot laced with LSD and went on a bad trip, the kind where you think you can fly and you take a running start and fall out an open window.

I wondered if Michael Strohman ever thought about me. Probably not, but if I was thinking about him, wasn't it possible he was thinking about me? One day I was in school and the next day I was gone forever. I pretended I was him and imagined how he might have felt. *Where's Blumberg?* he might have asked our English teacher, adding, *not that I care*. The teacher would have replied, *Billy's gone*, adding, *and none of you will ever see him again*. Michael Strohman would feel so guilty. *Oh man*, he'd say, rubbing one of the anti-war buttons on his cool army jacket. The very last time he saw me, he was kissing Pam Lowenstein in front of me. Now he felt sad—never *ever* to see a person again—but he couldn't cry or put his head down on his desk because that wouldn't be a Michael Strohman thing to do. He would pretend I never existed, but sometimes walking home from school, on that bridge over the creek, he would wonder why I disappeared and whether it had anything to do with him.

I turned off the television. I picked up an Agatha Christie book, *They Do It with Mirrors*. I read the first page, then snapped it shut and flipped it onto the floor. Michael Strohman was right—after reading enough of them, you really don't care who the killer is.

It was 4:15. I turned the television back on. *One Life to Live* was over and *Dark Shadows* was on. I didn't pay attention because I had my own soap opera running in my head: my dad, my mom, and Ms. Marvin. *Nancy, call me Nancy*, she said. Maybe my mind was snapping, just like Ms. Marvin had predicted it would. What if my mother found out that Ms. Marvin wrote the hex list and I had been to her apartment for the séance and I knew that my father might have been her boyfriend?

I had a terrifying thought, a new Official Worry that rocketed to the top of my list. I opened my closet door and started rummaging through a box of papers and assorted junk. I found it quickly, a long rolled-up photo with a rubber band around it—my sixth-grade class picture. I slid off the rubber band, unfurled the picture, and turned it over. And there it was, scrawled in dark purple ink:

To Billy, the fashion plate of the sixth grade—Nancy Marvin

My mother still had the hex list. What if she compared Ms. Marvin's handwriting on the picture with the handwriting on the hex list? It might match—those plump loops under the *g* and *f*, the curly way she crossed the *y* in *Billy*. Was it enough to prove, *conclusively*, that Ms. Marvin wrote the hex list?

There was a complete set of *World Book* encyclopedias in our living room. Was there a chapter on handwriting? I pulled the H volume from the bookshelf. I leafed through—it said, *Handwriting Analysis*, see: *Graphology*. I pulled the G volume. Graphology—a genuine scientific name like "geology" or "geography." This meant that people studied graphology in schools and universities, that graphologists in white suits conducted graphology experiments in laboratories.

I read the chapter. Graphology, it said, was so much more than comparing two samples of handwriting to see if they were written by the same person. According to graphology, you could find out everything about a person's personality by analyzing their handwriting. Things like the size of the letters and the "degree and regularity" of "slanting, ornamentation, angularity and curvature" allowed you to look into someone's soul and find out everything about them no matter how hard they tried to hide it.

I took the G volume to my room and laid it open next to the Ms. Marvin handwriting sample. The book contained a graphology chart that explained what different types of slanting and curving meant in a person. I carefully examined Ms. Marvin's handwriting: the letters were plump and curly. What did it mean? One sentence in the chart stood out. "A cursive *y* that has been crossed back over ornately or several times can indicate a perverted state of mind." *To Billy*, she had written on the back of the picture, the loop on the *y* with its little curl, crossing back and forth, definitely ornate. Therefore, according to this graphological analysis, Ms. Marvin definitely wrote the hex list and she had a perverted state of mind.

I heard a key in the lock. I snapped the *World Book* shut. The front door opened and my mother threw her keys onto the counter. "Billy?" she called out. "Are you here?"

"Of course," I called back. "Where else would I be?" I scrambled, rolling up the class picture and tossing it back in my closet. I went into the living room, still holding the G volume.

She took off her coat, then looked at me. "What did you do all day?"

"Nothing." Maybe, I thought, I should throw my class picture down the garbage chute tomorrow morning, thereby destroying the evidence against me. But didn't my mother have my sixth-grade report cards, all in Ms. Marvin's handwriting? I was doomed.

"Why are you carrying the *World Book*?" she asked.

"Um, I was looking up Georgia in America and Georgia in the Soviet Union. I was curious if they shared any characteristics aside from the name."

She blinked a few times. "Do they?" She looked tired.

"Turns out," I said, putting the G volume back on the bookshelf, "they don't."

WE ATE MACARONI AND CHEESE for dinner. It was the perfect dish for eating in silence—no embarrassing loud crunching or knives and forks clinking against plates. She hadn't asked about the hex list. I wasn't going to say anything because if I was still in trouble anything I said would just make it worse. All this silence was a good thing because I could concentrate on digesting my meal. I had seen a movie in science class about the human body. It said that 75% of your blood went to the brain, and the rest went either to your digestive system or to your muscles. This was why you weren't supposed to run around on a full stomach. So wouldn't having a big conversation while you eat dinner—which involves not only your brain but also your jaw muscles—divert the blood away from your digestive system while you're eating?

I cleaned my plate and poured myself another glass of juice.

"Would you like some more macaroni and cheese?" she asked.

"No thanks," I said. This was a safe conversation because it was short and required very little brain activity, leaving plenty of blood for the digestive system.

My mother took a deep breath, then said, "I need to talk to you about something."

I could feel my stomach stop digesting. She paused and stared at her plate, like she was thinking about what she was going to say and how she was going to say it. Had she already compared the handwriting samples? Why in a million years would you go over to Ms. Marvin's apartment, she would want to know. How could you betray your own mother?

But instead, she said, "I have a certain disease."

I waited while 100% of my blood throbbed in my forehead. "What?" I said.

"It's a brain disease called," she paused, like she was in a classroom about to write it on a blackboard, "multiple sclerosis."

"Is it the Jerry Lewis telethon disease?"

"No, that's muscular dystrophy."

"Is it Lou Gehrig's disease?"

"No."

"So, what is it?" I asked. Maybe I hadn't heard of it.

"It's a disease where your nerves don't work the right way."

"What does it feel like?"

"I'm tired all the time and my left side is numb."

"You're going to be okay, right?"

"Maybe. It could come and go. Or I could end up in a wheelchair for the rest of my life. Or worse."

"Or worse? What could be worse?"

"Billy . . ."

"How did you get it?"

"They don't know. It's a mystery."

I stared at my empty plate. If I had asked for seconds of macaroni and cheese, maybe this conversation wouldn't be happening.

"Look at me. What are you thinking?"

"It's my fault. For putting you on the hex list."

"It's *absolutely* not your fault," she said.

"How do you know?"

"Because all this business about some list causing bad things to happen to people is completely absurd."

"How do you know?"

"Listen to me, Billy. It's very important for you to believe that this is not your fault."

"But what if it is?"

"And what if it's not?" She stood up and walked over to her purse on the kitchen counter, then pulled out a folded-up piece of paper. My hex list. She spread it out on the table before us.

"I can't prove a negative," she said. "That means I can't prove something isn't true. But that doesn't mean it *is* true. You have to prove a positive. How do you know hexes *do* exist? Where is your proof?"

I held up five fingers and recited the entire body of evidence. One: Lawrence and Harold Feinbaum died in a car crash. Two: Brooks Robinson sprained his ankle. Three: Kurt Johnson's grandfather had a heart attack. Four: Mr. Pappas probably had a stroke. I left out the fifth one.

"All coincidences. Every single one," she said, pointing at the list. "What about this Michael Strohman boy. Anything happen to him?"

"I don't think so," I said. "He's back in Silver Spring."

"Meaning what? That the curse doesn't travel outside Rockville city limits?"

"Well, no," I said. "Brooks Robinson sprained his ankle in Florida."

"Then why would a hex affect one person on the list and not another person?"

"I don't know," I said. "There are things in the spirit world we humans don't understand."

My mother clicked her tongue. "So in other words, when something bad happens, you *know* it's caused by this hex, but when nothing happens, you just blame it on the spirit world being beyond your understanding? Do you understand how ridiculous that is?"

"No," I said.

"Why do you want to believe this? Do you want to believe that you caused me to get sick?"

"Of course not."

"So why do you want to believe in this hex list?" she said.

"I don't know."

But I did know. I wanted to believe my dad was floating in the spirit world, looking over me. *It's not like I care*, I had told him that morning. What were the magic words that would have changed his mind and made him decide that day not to kill himself? It's not like I *don't* care, I could have said. It's not like I meant to laugh when Harold Feinbaum threw the paper airplane and knocked your yarmulke off. It's not like I meant for Harold and his father to die in that car crash.

And it's not like I meant for my mother to get sick. I felt really bad. I had to tell her. "I have something to confess."

"Billy . . ."

"I'm really sorry."

"Billy . . ."

"I didn't mean for this to happen."

"I know," my mother said, softly.

"Know what?"

"I know that Marvin woman wrote the list."

"How do you know?"

"I just know."

"Why didn't you tell Mr. Dixon that Ms. Marvin did it?"

"It wouldn't have made any difference," she said. "You'd still be in trouble. And those people don't need to know our business."

I told my mother about the 7-Eleven, Ms. Marvin picking me up in Mr. Wilson's office, the voodoo masks on the wall, the black candle.

"Tell me *exactly* what that woman said." My mother spoke slowly, like she was trying to control herself.

"She said we needed to summon dad from the spirit world so he could put curses on the people on the list."

"Terrific," she said. "It's not enough that she . . ."

"Not enough that she what?"

"Never mind. I should report her to the police."

"Are hexes against the law?"

"No, they're not. And do you know why? Because they don't have laws against things that aren't real."

"Then why would you call the police?"

"I probably won't." She rubbed her eyes. "What was the name of your elementary school principal? Mr. Braxton?"

"No. Mr. Barton," I said. "Why?"

"Oh, no reason. Now, let's break this down," she said. "This woman wrote the names you gave her, and then she summoned your father from the spirit world to activate the curse. Is that how it works?"

"Pretty much."

"Pretty much? It's a yes or no question. Here's what you said. One: Ms. Marvin writes down the names you give her. Two: She summons your father from the spirit world. Three: Your father puts the curse on those people. *Is that how it works?*"

"Yes."

"But then . . . later you added my name yourself. Right?"

"A couple of days later. I didn't mean to. I was mad at you because you yelled at me during dinner. I didn't mean it. I'm sorry." She blinked and waved her hand like she was shooing away a fly.

"We're not talking about that now. The point is, when you added my name, your father's spirit wasn't 'summoned' and hovering around to activate the curse, right? So I don't understand how you can possibly think that putting my name on that list is responsible for me getting sick."

"Maybe Dad was checking on the list from the spirit world. So when I added your name . . ."

"That's ridiculous."

"I'll get the curse removed."

"No, you won't. There's nothing to remove."

"But what if there are things in the spirit world we humans don't understand?"

"There is no spirit world, Billy. People live, die, and that's it."

"How do you know?"

"I can't believe I'm having this discussion with you. Okay. Let's accept for the sake of argument that all this hex business is true. Why do you think your father would want me to get MS?"

I stared at the list, at her name in my handwriting all shaky and back-slanted, with the crisscrossings of a snapped mind.

"Maybe it's because he's brand new in the spirit world and he didn't know how to do things and he messed up something."

"Possible. But not likely."

"Maybe," I said, "it was supposed to be a much worse curse and he made it as good as possible."

"He couldn't do any better than multiple sclerosis? Thanks a lot."

"Because of him, you'll recover."

"Or maybe I won't. Maybe your Ms. Marvin turned him against me."

"She's not my Ms. Marvin. And he would never do that."

"No? You sure about that?"

"Yes."

"Because you knew him better than anyone, right?"

"Maybe. I don't know."

"Well, here's a little something you don't know. Your father left a kind of note."

"He did?" I said. "What did it say?"

"Hard to describe," she said. "Because it's not really a note, per se. It's something else with which you may have some familiarity."

She got up and went into her bedroom. I heard a drawer opening, the sounds of something being unfolded. This note that wasn't really a note—maybe it would hold a coded message only I would understand, a mysterious puzzle with which only I would have familiarity.

She came back into the kitchen and slapped it down on the table in front of me.

It was a list of names on his stationery, with the top imprinted "From the Desk of Murray Blumberg." *Harold Feinbaum, Rabbi Levine, Bob Short, Leonid Brezhnev, Richard Nixon.* It was written with those curly and ornate letters, an exact match with *To the fashion plate of the sixth grade—Nancy Marvin.*

And at the bottom of the list, my father had written his own name, a mad jumble of loops slightly edging downward. I tried to remember what the graphology chart said about all the angles and slants and loops but it was just too complicated.

. *12* .

Hawaii Is a Island in the Pacific

DAY TWO OF MY SUSPENSION. I decided to call Ms. Marvin on the telephone at 4:30 p.m. and ask her to remove the curse. The bell at Forest Glen Elementary rang at 3:00 p.m. and I assumed she would leave at 3:45, at the latest. How long did it take to erase blackboards and clean erasers? Then she had to drive home, from Silver Spring to Rockville. Twenty minutes, a half hour? That stretched it to 4:15. Then I had to give her fifteen minutes to take off her coat, go to the bathroom, maybe get a snack. Did grown-ups eat snacks in the afternoon? Cupcakes, candy, ice cream? They were like gods, allowed to eat anything.

I paced around the living room, talking to myself, making my plan. Maybe ten extra minutes for a snack. So 4:40. But my mother came home between 5:00 and 5:30, so I had to make the call as close to 4:40 as possible, in case our conversation lasted a long time. If I didn't do this, I would worry about it all afternoon, evening, and night and I wouldn't be able to sleep and I would go through this same torture tomorrow, on Day Three of my suspension. I looked at the clock on the kitchen wall. 4:33. If I stared hard at the minute hand, I could see it moving. The hour hand looked like a big fat thumb, stock still, pressing down hard. I went into my bedroom and looked at the clock on my dresser. 4:34. This clock was a squat red box with big white numbers that were on a wheel. When the minute changed, you could see the next number slowly slide into place, hear the low scratchy whine of gears turning and scraping. 4:36. 4:37. 4:38.

It was time for formal preparation. I tore out the piece of notebook paper on which I had written my questions. I went into the kitchen and placed the questions on the kitchen table. Then I filled a glass with water from the tap and positioned it next to the questions in case my mouth got dry or my voice got hoarse while I was on the phone. Then I sat down. Then I stood up. I picked up the phone on the kitchen counter. The cord was long enough so I could sit at the table and look at my questions and drink my water. I looked at the kitchen clock. 4:39 and 30 seconds. Too soon? I placed the receiver back on its hook and reviewed my questions:

Questions for Mike Epstein

Can you remove the thing, especially the one on Ed Brinkman, even though I'm the one who actually did that particular one?

If the answer is YES: Do you need the actual original list to remove the thing?

If the answer is YES, actually this could be a problem, since Ed Brinkman keeps it in ~~her~~ his purse.

If the answer is NO: What am I supposed to do?

Why would Frank Howard put the thing on himself by writing his own name on his own list?

The questions were in code in case my mother found this particular piece of notebook paper. Every time I wrote stuff down—the hex list, the letter to Julie Baines—it ended up in the wrong hands and I got in trouble. My mother wouldn't know the code because I used the names of Washington Senator baseball players and she hated baseball.

4:41. Was it too late? Had the window of opportunity closed? I jerked to my feet, grabbed the receiver, and dialed O for operator. I heard two rings, then:

"Operator. How can I help you?" I had never talked to a telephone operator before. She didn't sound anything like Ernestine from *Laugh-In.*

"Would you please connect me to the Nancy Marvin residence?" I whispered.

"I'm sorry, I can't hear you. You need to speak louder."

"Would you connect me to the Nancy Marvin residence?"

"What city?"

"Rockville."

"I have an N. Marvin in Rockville. Would you like me to connect you?"

"Is N. Marvin a man . . . ," I asked, ". . . or a lady?"

"Would you like me to connect you?"

"I guess so."

"One moment, please." I heard a phone ringing on the other end of the line. What if it was the wrong N. Marvin? Nathan or Nora or Neil?

The phone kept ringing. Three times, four times, five times.

Holding the receiver tight against my ear, I sat down at the kitchen table and looked at my questions. The code was brilliant. Mike Epstein was Ms. Marvin, Ed Brinkman was my mother, and Frank Howard was my father. The "thing" was the hex or the curse. But why had I used the word "list"? I should have thought of a code word for "list" too. "Item" would have been perfect. *Do you need the actual original item to remove the thing?* I should have written it that way.

The phone rang, seven times, eight times, nine times.

What if the right N. Marvin answered? Was she one of those people who just picks up the phone and says "hello?" or would she say something like "Marvin residence"? What should I say? "Is this Nancy?" She had said, "Call me Nancy."

The phone kept ringing. I imagined her hand reaching for the receiver, her lungs breathing, her heart beating. *Hello*, she would say. Maybe right now, at this very moment, Ms. Marvin was outside in the hallway and she heard it ringing from inside her apartment. Maybe she had a boyfriend, some teacher at school or Mr. Wilson or the father of one of her favorite students, and what if he hadn't called her in a really long time, and she heard the phone and she just knew it was him. So when she hears the phone ringing in the hallway, she has to rush to answer it, because he might not bother calling her again and she knows that every wasted second makes it more likely that when she finally picks up the phone and says hello, she'll hear that click and dead air and she'll have missed that call forever.

Twenty-five, twenty-six, twenty-seven rings. Could phones ring forever? What if there was a phone call where some guy calls some girl and right before she answers, the planet Jupiter explodes and bombards the earth with gamma rays that instantaneously kill every living being on Earth. But say that electricity is impervious to gamma rays, so the phone keeps ringing. It rings for 5,000, 6,000, 7,000 years, and then one day alien archeologists from another galaxy visit Earth. And this one alien levitates down the hallway and he hears a phone ringing from inside the apartment. So he blasts open the door with an electromagnetic matter-antimatter disrupter and runs inside. He jumps over the girl's dress on the floor, now filled with the dust of her bones. The alien archeologist picks up the phone and says, "Hello?" His alien face—two noses, two mouths, one big eye—is shocked at what he hears on the phone. The End.

I hung up. I looked at the *Questions for Mike Epstein*. Now I had two more questions, but these were for myself. What was wrong with me? And when was I going to grow up? I crossed out the questions with my black felt-tip pen, layer upon layer of thick black obliterating ink. Then I wrote down the only question I really wanted to ask.

AT 2:00 P.M. ON DAY THREE of my suspension, I snuck past the front desk and walked three blocks to the bus stop in downtown Rockville. The sidewalks were empty. A cold gust of wind rattled the trees. An old lady with a pinched and worried look sat at the bus stop, clutching an umbrella and a plastic bag.

"Um, excuse me, ma'am," I said, trying to smile and look friendly. Maybe I would remind her of her grandson and she would be nice to me. "Could you tell me which of the buses go down University Boulevard to Silver Spring?"

She looked at my face, then my hands, then my face again. "The Q-2," she said.

"How much does it cost?" I asked.

"Forty cents."

"*Thank you* very much," I said, practically bowing.

She frowned. "Why aren't you in school?"

"What?" I said. I tried to look confused. Maybe she would think I was brain-addled and leave me alone.

"Why are you *not* in school?"

"Well," I said. "We just moved here from Alaska and I start my new school tomorrow and my mother told me I need to go to Silver Spring to buy school supplies."

"*Alaska*?"

"Yes ma'am," I said. "Land of the Midnight Sun."

"Where in Alaska?"

"Um . . . Juneau." Thank God I had memorized all the state capitals in the fifth grade.

"Where's your mother?"

"She's working," I said. "At her new job." I looked down the street and saw a bus coming, about two blocks away. It said *Q-2, Silver Spring*.

"Where does your mother work?"

"In an office."

"Which office?" The bus was now a half block away.

"Some government office downtown," I said. "It's kind of classified."

The bus pulled up. The lady pointed across the street toward the shopping center. "You can buy all the school supplies you want at Grants. Why do you have to go all the way to Silver Spring?"

"I don't know," I said. The doors opened and I climbed on. I fumbled through my pocket for a quarter, a dime, and a nickel. I would have had my forty cents ready if it weren't for that old busybody. Why couldn't people mind their own business? I kept fumbling. The bus driver frowned at me. He had dark scary eyes and hairy knuckles that gripped the steering wheel. I gathered the correct change and put it in the box. Then the bus lurched forward. I staggered down the aisle and sat down as far away from other people as I could get. What if that old lady called the school and the school called the police and the police radioed the bus driver? I looked out the window at the Suburban Trust bank clock. 2:15. It was Norway. *Norway* was the "Land of the Midnight Sun."

We passed Richard Montgomery, the high school I would be going to someday if I lived that long and if we stayed in Rockville and if I didn't have to go to reform school for the rest of my life. At the radio station building, WINX 1600 AM, the bus turned onto Veirs Mill Road, which went all the way to Wheaton. I looked out the window at a McDonald's, "Over 15 Million Served." This was really happening. I was a horrible person. My father was dead and it may have been my fault. I had put a terrible hex on people who actually died. I was suspended from school. I was going to have a Thursday bar mitzvah. I had snuck away against the wishes of my mother who, because of the hex list, was probably dying of some kind of Lou Gehrig's disease.

The bus kept stopping and starting, starting and stopping. My tooth hurt. My head hurt, a nervous tension headache they always talked about in the Anacin commercials. I could feel the nervous tension flowing through my nervous system down into my stomach. We passed through Wheaton and turned down University Boulevard. We were getting close. My elementary school, Forest Glen, was on University Boulevard near Dennis Avenue. But now I had a new worry. How was I supposed to know when we got to Dennis Avenue? I was worried the bus would pass Dennis Avenue and I would miss it. Passengers on the bus were pulling the string to get off, but you had to do it about half a block before the bus got there. Should I go up to the front of the bus and ask the bus driver? There was a sign that said *Do not talk to the driver while this bus is in operation.* On the one hand, he stopped at stoplights and when he picked up or dropped off somebody. Maybe I could talk to him then? But on the other hand, when he was stopped at a stoplight, wasn't the bus still "in operation?"

We kept going down University Boulevard passing all sorts of streets—Warren Street, Nicholas Drive, Louis Place. My father once told me they took street names from the street builders' relatives. So in other words, maybe the guy who built Dennis Avenue had a son named Dennis. I wondered what it was like to have a street named after you. What if there was a Billy Street? On the plus side, I'd be a celebrity. I'd stop people on my street and say "hello, I'm Billy." Then I'd pause and say, "*the* Billy." On the minus side, there would be lots of pressure not to screw up on that particular street. You might embarrass your father and he'd be sorry he named the street after you.

I looked out the window and saw the sign "Dennis Avenue" go whizzing by. I panicked. I ran up to the front of the bus and said to the bus driver while the bus was in operation, "Um, excuse me, I needed to get off at Dennis Avenue."

"Why the hell didn't you tell me?" the bus driver said, eyes on the road, his hands cradling an enormous steering wheel, as big as a platter. I was glad he couldn't look at me.

"I'm sorry," I said.

"Just get off at the next stop and walk back. Jesus Christ."

The bus lurched to a stop and he let me off. I started walking back toward Dennis Avenue when I saw, from across a blacktop, three kids sitting around a picnic table under a tree. One of the kids had his back to me, but I could see he was wearing an army jacket with anti-war buttons. He had long black curly hair that fell over his shoulders. He was slouching over the table and moving his hands as he talked to the other two kids.

It was Michael Strohman. Definitely. He was probably conducting a "teach-in" about the injustice of the war in Southeast Asia. I was too far away to get a good look at his face, but I knew it was him.

Then it hit me. The spirit world *made* me miss the Dennis Avenue stop and put me on the corner of University Boulevard and Lorain Avenue at 2:45 p.m. because I was *supposed* to see Michael Strohman. It was Michael Strohman and *not Ms. Marvin* I was meant to see on this trip because if it weren't for Michael Strohman inviting me to that anti-war rally in Sligo Park, I wouldn't have been mad at my father for having to instead go to Hebrew school and I wouldn't have laughed at him when he got his yarmulke knocked off and maybe he wouldn't have killed himself.

I heard Michael Strohman say something and the other two kids at the picnic table laughed. Michael Strohman was on my hex list, but it looked like nothing bad had happened to him and wouldn't that mean he had greater powers than Ms. Marvin? And now I was supposed to go up to Michael Strohman and Michael Strohman was supposed to say something to me that would explain everything and solve all my problems. I felt the nervous tension rising in my head, stomach, and right shoulder as I crossed the blacktop toward the picnic table. Michael Strohman was still talking to the other kids. I thought I heard him say "DMZ." These Sligo kids were so much cooler than the idiots at my new school. At Sligo, people talked about Cambodia and Nixon and the Paris Peace Talks, while at West Montgomery people just talked about whether kid A could beat up kid B.

I reached the end of the blacktop and came up behind the picnic table, my feet crunching the dead leaves. The two kids looked at me while Michael Strohman continued to talk.

"*DMZ?*" I said to Michael Strohman's back, "*Demilitarized zone!*" This was going to be an emotional reunion.

The guy in the army jacket turned around. It wasn't Michael Strohman.

"*What?*" he said. He and his two friends were bigger than they had looked from a distance. Ninth graders, probably.

"Who the fuck are you?" the not-Michael Strohman said.

"Nobody," I said. "I thought you were someone else. I'm sorry."

"Who did you think I was?"

"Michael Strohman," I said. "Do you know him?"

"Maybe."

It figured that Michael Strohman would know a ninth grader. Maybe they went to anti-war protest demonstrations together.

"Is he okay?"

"Is who okay?"

"Michael Strohman."

"How the fuck should I know?"

Maybe this was a sign. I was not supposed to know what happened to Michael Strohman. Maybe he had no friends and wandered the halls of Sligo alone and got D's on his social studies projects. Or maybe he was still the coolest and smartest kid in the seventh grade and was still kissing Pam Lowenstein on a picnic bench in Sligo Park. It was another mystery I would never solve.

"You got any pot?" said one of the other kids.

"No."

"Got any cigarettes?"

"No."

"Got any money?"

"Um, no."

"Empty your pockets," said the fake Michael Strohman. He went behind me and grabbed the back of my neck.

I pulled out a handful of change from my pocket.

"What's your name?"

"Billy."

"Can you loan me some money, Billy?" he said. "I swear to God I'll pay it back."

I handed over all of it.

"Now get the fuck out of here," he said, letting go of my neck and pushing me to the ground. I got up and ran and heard them all laughing.

I ran for about a block and stopped when I got tired. The palms of my hands stung from landing hard on the gravelly dirt. I was shaking all over. When people talked about getting mugged is this what they were talking about? I dug into my pants pocket and pulled out what was left, one nickel and six pennies. Why did I have to give them all my quarters and dimes? How was I going to get home?

It was 2:50. I reached Dennis Avenue and crossed University Boulevard at the traffic light. I reached the parking lot of Forest Glen Elementary. My plan was to wait for Ms. Marvin next to her car, the Volkswagen I remembered from the time she gave me the ride to her apartment. I crossed the parking lot, looking at all the teachers' cars. Then I saw it, that yellow VW Bug. It had a bumper sticker that said *Maryland is for Crabs.* I sat down on a grassy ridge in front of the car and waited.

At 2:53, the front doors of Forest Glen opened and out came the safety patrols, about eight sixth graders wearing their yellow belts down across the shoulder and around the waist, their bright badges glistening in the sunlight. They fanned out in different directions. Being a safety patrol was a big deal because you got to leave school before everybody else and you got to act like you were a cop and boss around little kids crossing the streets. I could have been a safety patrol, but I said no because you had to get up earlier, get home later, and you had to tie your belt around your badge in an official way, like you were tying a tie. You had to practice and show them you could do it right. I wasn't interested.

At 3:00, the bell rang. There were a few minutes of silence, then the doors opened and kids came out, running, walking, shouting. A few looked in my direction, then looked away. Some faces looked familiar, but I had never known the kids in the grades behind me. I felt like a ghost.

"Billy? Billy Blumberg?" I heard from behind me.

I turned around and it was Mrs. Lewis, my fifth-grade teacher. Great. I was looking for my sixth-grade teacher and I got my fifth-grade teacher. Mrs. Lewis looked a lot older than I remember, her face fatter, her hair grayer.

"How are you, Billy?" she said, not quite smiling.

"Fine."

"I heard about your father," she said. "I'm really sorry."

"Thanks." She looked at me, her eyes narrowing.

"What are you doing here?"

"Nothing." She couldn't do anything, could she? I was in junior high and she was only an elementary school teacher. I was outside of her authority. It was like if I went to France the French police wouldn't have the power to do anything to me because I was an American. Isn't that how it worked?

"Shouldn't you be at school?" she asked. Junior high, not elementary school. Junior high. Not her territory. What was wrong with her?

"I'm in junior high."

"I know that. Sligo lets out later. Why aren't you there?"

"Well, we're doing a creative writing assignment for English class where they let us out early and we were supposed to go back to our elementary school and write a poem about it."

"Tell me the truth."

"It's junior high! Those are the kind of assignments you get!"

"Then where is everybody else in your class?"

"I don't go to Sligo anymore. We moved to Rockville."

"Billy . . ."

"It's true!"

She looked at her car and sighed. "Okay. We're going to go into the office and we're going to call your mom."

Should I run? She was really old and would never catch me. Or maybe I could make a deal with her and tell her that if she was so interested in rounding up junior high students cutting class, I knew where three of them were right now.

"Let's go inside to the office," Mrs. Lewis said. "I don't have time to fool around."

Then I heard a voice behind me say, "I've got this one, Janet. Go on home."

It was Ms. Marvin, watching us. She looked younger than I remembered.

"Are you sure, Nancy?" Mrs. Lewis said.

"Absolutely. I'm very familiar with Mr. Blumberg's situation," Ms. Marvin said, smiling at me. Silently, we watched Mrs. Lewis walk away. In Mrs. Lewis's class we had to write a report on a state. I did Hawaii. I wrote that "Hawaii is a island in the Pacific" rather than "Hawaii is *an* island in the Pacific." For that one mistake, she gave me an A-minus instead of an A. My father pointed out that it was actually a different mistake because Hawaii was a *bunch* of islands in the Pacific, not just *an* island, and that she missed the bigger mistake and I was lucky she didn't give me a B, all things considered. "Here's the point," he said. "Don't miss what's really important."

As soon as Mrs. Lewis was gone, Ms. Marvin turned to me. She wasn't smiling anymore.

"What are you doing here?"

I didn't need to look at my little piece of notebook paper, because I had memorized the question. It wasn't in code.

"Why did my father kill himself?" I asked.

. *13* .

Yellow Candle, Chocolate Cupcake

WHEN I GOT HOME from school on that day, there were police cars and an ambulance in front of our house. A policeman sat at the foot of our front steps. I unlatched the gate and walked down the brick pathway, eyes fixed on our front door, pretending that this cop sitting in front of my house was none of my concern and I was just going about my business. But as I reached the front steps, he stood up and moved in front of me.

"Hey bud," he said, eyes wide, a fake smile. His nametag said "Gordon." He had curly hair and a broad friendly face, kind of like Artemus Gordon who was always joking around and putting on goofy disguises on my third favorite television show of all time, *The Wild Wild West*. This Gordon stared at me, his smile fading.

"What's your name?" he said. He had a walkie-talkie on one hip and a holstered gun on the other.

"Billy," I said.

"Billy what?"

"Billy Blumberg."

He nodded like I had just given him the right answer. What was going on?

"Don't worry, you're not in trouble," Officer Gordon said. "You didn't do anything wrong."

We stared at each other.

"How was school today?" he said.

"Fine," I said.

"What grade are you in?"

"Seventh."

I heard that loud gasping sob coming from inside our house. My mother. *My stupid mother.*

"WHY DID MY FATHER KILL HIMSELF?" I asked Ms. Marvin in the parking lot of Forest Glen Elementary School.

"Get in," she said, unlocking and opening the passenger door. She scooped a pile of manila folders from the front and chucked it onto the back seat with a loud thump. I climbed in and put on my seat belt.

We pulled onto University Boulevard, the car rumbling. She gripped the steering wheel hard and I could see the white on her knuckles. She didn't say anything. Was she thinking about how to answer my question? Maybe I should have asked something else first—like "how's it going" or "what's new"—and then try to build up to the harder questions.

"So," she said, as we sat in a long line of traffic at a stoplight in downtown Wheaton. "I know you got suspended. And I know why you got suspended."

"Really?" How could she possibly know? Did she get a message from my dad in the spirit world? Did he tell her I would show up outside Forest Glen Elementary on December 2, 1971, at 3:07 p.m.? Then it hit me. It was her spy, Mr. Wilson. He must have watched me being marched in and out of Mr. Dixon's office.

The car started moving. She looked at me, then straight ahead. "Did you tell Vice Principal Dixon that I helped you with the hex list?"

"No."

"That's good," she said. "Because if you did, the hex will turn on you. Do you remember I told you that?"

"Yes."

"So you're not going to tell anybody. Right?"

"Right."

Technically, that wasn't a lie. I wouldn't have to tell anybody *in the future* because everybody either knew or was about to know. My mother and Kurt Johnson knew. Julie Baines kind of knew. All of West Montgomery Junior High knew about the hex list and Kurt would probably tell everybody that Ms. Marvin did it. The students, teachers, cafeteria ladies, and janitors would all learn the truth. They would tell their families and neighbors. The story of Ms. Marvin would blanket Rockville like a thick black cloud before spreading throughout the Washington Metropolitan Area. Maybe it would be on Channel 9 Eyewitness News. Did that mean the curse on myself would be even worse than it already was? How did it work? Maybe once you're already cursed it doesn't get worse or better, it just is. Or maybe telling lots of people would reverse the curse because a negative times a negative is a positive. There were so many possibilities.

We kept driving. Ms. Marvin seemed to relax a little. "Let's change the subject," she said. "I will tell you about my day. You're stuck in this car with me so you have to pay attention. And when I finish you have to ask me questions showing me that you have listened with great care and sensitivity. Are you ready?"

"I guess so."

"Well . . . ," she said. She talked fast—some boring story about getting in trouble with her boss, Mr. Barton, because she got to work fifteen minutes late and how he was out to "get" her, and when she went to the teachers union, they said there was nothing they could do.

"Now ask me a question," she said. "That shows you care."

"Like what?" I said.

"That's up to you."

"I can't think of anything," I said. That was a lie. I could think of plenty of questions. I was the Albert Einstein of questions. They came to me when I blinked my eyes, when I heard houses settling and telephones ringing, when I shoveled macaroni and cheese into my mouth. Thinking up questions about Ms. Marvin's stupid story—that was easy. Number One: Why was she fifteen minutes late to work? Number Two: Why was Mr. Barton out to "get" her? And bonus question Number Three: If she wasn't a teacher would there be another job where you could be fifteen minutes late and not get in trouble? All of those questions might have showed that I cared.

But I didn't care. I had different kinds of questions and I had asked the most important one and she hadn't answered. Should I ask it again? Maybe later. It was better that she concentrated on her driving. If she did answer it, she might get all sad and weepy and those white knuckles would come off the steering wheel to wipe the tears from her eyes and we'd slam into a telephone pole. She would be impaled on the steering wheel and then just as she whispered, *your father killed himself because . . .*, she would die right then and there and I would never know the truth.

"Asking caring and sensitive questions is important to a

healthy relationship," she said. "I'm teaching you a valuable lesson for when you grow up and have a nice little wife who needs to feel better about herself."

"I'm never getting married," I said.

"Ha! That's what they all say."

I wondered if my father asked Ms. Marvin caring and sensitive questions that showed he cared. Was he just *showing* he cared or did he really care? Did they *do it*, my father and Ms. Marvin? She was so crazy she probably would tell me if I asked and I didn't want to hear about it. He was a Hebrew school principal, which was one step below a rabbi. My father might have broken one of the Ten Commandments: *Thou shalt not commit adultery*. When I was a little kid, I thought adultery meant that you weren't supposed to act like an adult and do things like smoke cigarettes or drink beer or sneak into X-rated movies. But now I knew what it really meant.

"Can you reverse the hex I put on all those people?" I asked.

"No. I don't have the power to do that."

"Well maybe we can do another séance? Maybe we could ask my dad's ghost to reverse the hex."

"No, Billy."

"My mom's really sick," I said, my voice cracking just a little. "I added her name."

"I'm sorry. But we're not doing another séance."

"Why not?"

"Because I said so. I'm driving you home."

Again, she tightened her grip on the steering wheel. The car in front of us was a white Cadillac with fins, license plate Maryland CK115. The license plate on my father's car was CK112. He had a formula for remembering it. "CK" stood for chicken Kentucky, which was from Kentucky Fried Chicken. "11" was the eleven herbs and spices in the secret recipe of Colonel Sanders. And—my favorite part—"two" was the number after "one." *Remember this code and you will never forget this license plate*, he would tell me. *Sixty years from now, you'll be a grandfather and I'll be long gone, but you will still remember: CK112.*

CK112, CK112, CK112, I said in my head. Was this the message from my father that I could contact him to remove the hex? We passed the sign on Veirs Mill Road that said WELCOME TO ROCKVILLE, ALL-AMERICAN CITY. If he hadn't killed himself, wouldn't I still live in Silver Spring and go to Sligo and have friends? *CK112. CK112.* Maybe that would be enough to conjure his spirit before me. *Why did you do it?* I would say to him, his spirit floating in front of me, fuzzy, like bad TV reception. *Why did you do it?* Define "why," he would say. Define "you," define "do," define "it."

I'd rephrase my question. Why did you, Murray K. Blumberg, kill yourself in the middle of a bright sunny October day? And he might say he got too close to the "other side," and when you see things in the spirit world no mortal human ex-Hebrew school principal is supposed to see, well, it's like looking at the sun during an eclipse until you go blind, only in this case you're looking behind the door marked *Authorized Personnel Only* into that forbidden teachers' lounge of the spirits, and if you look hard enough your mind snaps.

We passed by the Rockville radio station, WINX. Almost home.

"CK112," I said out loud.

"What?" Ms. Marvin said. We were sitting at a stoplight.

"I have a question that shows how much I care," I said. "How much trouble would you get into if Principal Barton found out about the hex?"

"You don't need to worry about that. You need to worry that if you tell anybody, you will be cursed," she said.

"I don't care about that anymore," I said. "We have to do another séance. Or I'll tell."

"No, you won't."

"Yes, I will."

She stared straight ahead. The light turned green. The car behind us honked. She stomped on the gas pedal.

"Okay, fine. Just for a little while," she said, "and then I'll drive you home."

We pulled into her apartment garage. She parked and grabbed the folders from the back seat. We went up in the elevator. There was no talking like before, when she was telling me about past lives. I stared at the floor. Michael Strohman had asked me if I ever wondered where I belonged. Was it here? Trapped in an elevator with Ms. Marvin, who talked about minds snapping and laughed at blood gushing? I was blackmailing her and wasn't murdering blackmailers the number one motive in Agatha Christie mysteries?

The elevator doors opened. We walked down the long hallway to apartment 714. She put her key in the lock and twisted.

"Did some old lady used to live here?" I asked.

"Of course not," she said. "Keep quiet until we get inside."

Maybe Mr. Wilson would be waiting for me on the other side of the door and he would bludgeon me with his *Virginia is for Lovers* coffee cup. They would grab my arms and legs and carry me out into the hallway and throw my body down the garbage chute. Maybe I deserved that.

Her apartment was different than before. There were no weird paintings and drawings on the walls, no bug-eyed wooden dolls. Just a sofa and a coffee table and a TV. In the dining room was the same round table where we held the séance, but no dark red tablecloth, just dark shiny wood reflecting the light on the ceiling.

And no Mr. Wilson.

"What happened to the voodoo dolls?" I asked her.

"I've redecorated," she said. "It's what grown-ups do." I didn't see the cat either, but I was afraid to ask.

She pointed at the table. "Sit down." She said it the same way she had said "get in" when we were in the school parking lot. I pulled one of the chairs back and sat, putting the palms of my hands against the cool wood of the tabletop.

Ms. Marvin sat down across from me. She looked tired. "Now what?" she said.

"Why did my father kill himself?" I asked.

"I don't know, Billy. Nobody knows. Here's what's going to happen. We'll perform the séance, remove the hex, and then I'll take you home. Agreed?"

"No. I want you to *reverse* the hex," I said. "Removing's not good enough. Harold and Lawrence Feinbaum are already dead. Can you bring them back to life?"

"Of course not. Do you think I would be an elementary school teacher if I could bring dead people back to life?"

"But you can get my dad to reverse the hex so that people who are sick like my mom will get better, right?"

"Um . . . right," she said. She spread her hands flat against the table and closed her eyes. "Here we go."

"Don't we need a black candle?" I asked. "Like last time?"

"I don't have any of those candles anymore."

"How will it work without a candle?"

"Fine. I have other candles. Hold on a second."

She got up and went into the kitchen. I looked out the window and realized that Kurt Johnson and I had visited the *wrong apartment building* when we were trying to get Ms. Marvin to reverse the hex on him. We went to the one across the street. All these stupid Rockville high-rise apartment buildings looked the same.

From the kitchen, I heard a drawer sliding, a package opening, some plastic crinkling. She returned with a skinny yellow birthday candle stuck into a Hostess chocolate cupcake.

"Will this really work?"

"Absolutely," she said. "First of all, I don't have a candle holder for such a small candle, so I had to stick it in a cupcake. And actually, because we're removing, I mean *reversing* the hex, the last thing we need is a black candle, and as a matter of fact, yellow is perfect because yellow is, you know, sunshine, growth . . . photosynthesis. And a birthday candle is perfect because it symbolizes positivity, new beginnings, revitalization. And you may eat the cupcake when we finish and then I can drive you home. Do you want a glass of milk?"

"Of course not." She didn't even know that ever since my father killed himself, I *hated* milk, that I didn't even pour it on my cereal in the morning.

"Okay. Do you have the hex list?"

"No. My mother confiscated it."

"That doesn't matter," she said. "Just write the names down on a piece of paper."

"We don't need the original list?"

"No, this list will *symbolize* the original list."

"You mean like a yellow birthday candle symbolizes photosynthesis?"

"Exactly."

She got up and brought back an ashtray, a piece of notebook

paper, and a pen. I wrote the names: *Harold Feinbaum, Lawrence Feinbaum, Bob Short, Brooks Robinson, Mr. Pappas, Kurt Johnson, Bob King, Stephen Danielson, Julie Baines, Michael Strohman. My stupid mother*. I drew a line through *Julie Baines.* I drew a line through *stupid.*

She struck a match and lit the skinny yellow birthday candle. "Stare into the flame. Then close your eyes and see the flame in your mind."

I closed my eyes and saw the flame against the darkness of my closed eyelids. I wanted to know what evil thing my father saw on the other side and what made him do it. He probably wouldn't want to tell me because it might make my mind snap too. But I would tell him that whatever it was, I wanted to know, and I would be careful enough to keep that horrible truth, whatever it was, from driving me crazy. It would be like cutting a little hole in a cardboard box and projecting an eclipse onto a smooth piece of sidewalk, next to the dirty scuff marks and the flattened paper cups and the bird shit.

"Now open your eyes."

She took the piece of paper with the list, crumpled it up, and put it into the ashtray. Then she lifted the cupcake and tilted the lit candle into the paper. The paper flared, then darkened and shriveled into black ash.

"Now blow out the flame."

I blew out the candle.

"It is done," she said.

It felt like nothing had happened.

"The hex is completely reversed," she said. "Your mother should get better, but if she doesn't, it's not anybody's fault. Sometimes people get sick for no reason."

"But didn't she get sick when the hex was on her?"

"Perhaps, but now that the hex is reversed, it didn't have anything to do with her getting sick. Now I'm going to drive you home. You can take the cupcake with you in the car." She stood up quickly, her chair scraping backwards against the floor.

"No," I said, watching a few teardrops of yellow wax harden on the surface of the cupcake icing. "I want you to summon my father's spirit."

"We just did, Billy. He reversed the hex, like I said."

Did she think I was stupid? "No. I want you to summon him so I can talk to him."

"I'm not going to do that, Billy."

"Why not?"

"Because I said so. I'm driving you home now. Let's go."

"You're not my teacher anymore. I don't have to listen to you."

"Oh yes, you do. I'm a teacher and you're a pupil in the Montgomery County Public School System. You have to do what I say."

"But I'm suspended. So technically, at this very moment, I'm not a pupil in the Montgomery County School System."

"Nice try," she said, laughing. It was a mean laugh.

"So . . . if your boss finds out about the hex, will you get fired?"

"Watch it."

"Will you?"

She blinked and sat back down at the table. She relit the candle on the cupcake and snapped her fingers. The light overhead seemed to flicker. Or was it just my imagination? I felt my heart trying to jump out of my chest.

"I sense his presence, Billy. His spirit is at peace."

"What's he saying?" I asked.

"Your father is very happy living in the spiritual world. He says he loves you a lot and that what happened wasn't your fault. And he has reversed the hex. He said to tell you it's reversed and you shouldn't worry about it anymore."

"What else?"

"He misses you very much," she said, closing her eyes, then opening them like she had just received a transmission. I couldn't see him or hear him, but I thought that maybe I sort of felt him, the way you feel like something is about to happen. But on the other hand, what he said didn't really sound like him. He probably would have made a joke about the cupcake.

"Ask him," I said, "why he killed himself."

"He can't answer a question like that."

"Why not?"

"It just doesn't work that way."

"Well, why not just ask him and see what he says?"

"We have to be careful not to ask him things that will scare him away forever. You don't want that, do you?"

"No." What I wanted was to hear about evil fire-spewing spirits, about two-headed, three-eyed, eight-tentacled monsters that snapped his mind into pieces and made him write his own name on his own hex list. What I wanted to hear was that me laughing at a paper airplane popping off his yarmulke in Hebrew school class had nothing to do with it.

"You have to ask appropriate questions," she said.

"How about this. Why *didn't* he kill himself? What were some reasons a person might think he did it which actually had nothing to do with it?"

"Billy," she said, shaking her head. "I can feel his spirit slipping away. This may be a good time to end this."

"Okay, wait. Does he remember things about his life on earth?"

She paused. "Sure. Some things."

"What was his license plate number?"

"He's not going to remember things like license plate numbers."

"Does he remember my name?"

"Of course."

"Does he remember the day I was born?"

"Yes."

"What day of the week was it?"

She shifted in her chair. "The spirits don't remember things like dates and numbers and facts. Your father remembers when you were born and he remembers how he felt. Spirits especially remember feelings and emotions."

"How did he feel when I was born?"

"He felt very very happy."

"Is that what he just said? 'Very very happy?' Why can't you just repeat what he says, word-for-word, so it's like I'm talking to him?"

"It doesn't work that way."

"How does it work?"

"Look, I can't repeat exactly what he says because I don't hear his voice in my head, okay? I sense the essence of his spirit in response to your questions and then I try to translate for you. Do you understand?"

"Does he remember my mother?"

"Yes. Of course."

"How does he feel about her?"

She paused again. "Uh, it's complicated."

"Is that what he said? 'It's complicated'?"

"No, that's the essence of how he feels about that particular question, Billy."

"What does 'it's complicated' mean?"

"I don't know."

"Can you ask him?"

"No," she said.

"Is 'it's complicated' how he feels about the question I asked or how he feels about my mother or both?"

"I sense that your father is getting impatient with all these questions." Really? My father would love all these questions. Weren't these the questions that he himself would ask, with that twinkle in his eye?

"So . . . when I wrote my mother's name on the hex list, was he forced to give my mother multiple sclerosis, or is it something he didn't mind doing anyway?"

"That's enough questions. This isn't *Jeopardy*."

"Of course not. In *Jeopardy* you get the answers and you have to give the questions. Like for example, '*Love Story*.'"

"What about it?"

"The correct response would be: What was the movie we went to see on Labor Day weekend when he got into a big fight with my mother in the car? Does he remember that?"

"I don't know, Billy."

"You don't know or he doesn't remember?"

She closed her eyes and rubbed her forehead. "Yes, he remembers that."

"Okay," I said. "Okay. Does he remember how he *felt* during that fight?"

"Yes," she said. "He felt sad."

"Now. What was the name of the Ali MacGraw character in the *Mad Magazine* satire?"

"He's not going to remember that, Billy."

"Yes, he will!" I shouted. "I was in the back seat and I said it *during* the fight and he thought it was really funny. Doesn't thinking something is funny make you happy and isn't being happy a feeling? *Ask him.* What was the name of the Ali MacGraw character in the *Mad Magazine* satire?"

"I'm not going to ask him that."

"Yes, but he, I mean, you Dad, would know that because remember the time we went to see *Love Story* and I told you and you thought it was really funny?"

"You can't ask him questions like that because once he gets in the spirit world all the trivialities of human existence disappear and it's only the important things that remain."

"But this is important!" I said.

"It's not."

"I'll give you a hint, Dad. Cowsnowski . . ."

"Billy. No."

". . . Bumstein. Cowsnowski-Bumstein. What's the rest of it?"

"Stop."

"Pasta . . . It has to be coming back. I've practically given you the whole name!"

"Stop it."

"Foozala! Foozala!" I screamed. "Cowsnowski-Bumstein-Pastafoozala! He would never forget that! Ever."

I blew out the yellow candle on the chocolate cupcake. She looked at her watch. I looked at mine. It was 5:30 and my mother was already home and looking for me. I had disappeared and Ms. Marvin was the prime suspect. Maybe my mom had already called the police. Maybe she had already called Principal Barton.

"Time to go," Ms. Marvin said. She looked dejected. "It's all over."

I didn't need the spirit world to help me predict the future. Ms. Marvin would be fired and I would never see her again. My suspension would end and I would return to the seventh grade and keep going. And maybe . . . if I thought things would get better, they would.

My father had left us, but would I ever know the reason why? Was he in the spirit world or was he gone forever? And why did I miss him and love him and hate him all at the same time?

So many questions.

Epilogue

My father's yahrzeit candle burns through the night. On Yom Kippur, my mother will join him in the kitchen sink. She passed away fifteen years ago, having lived with her multiple sclerosis, but never letting it stop her. She was my hero.

In the morning, I eat breakfast while my wife sleeps. Cheerios with no milk, dry, the way my father liked it. He and I used to have long conversations about the kinds of breakfasts a President of the United States might eat. Is it predetermined, or can the President pad downstairs in his pajamas to the White House kitchen and order anything he wants? Smoked sturgeon, for example. Blood pudding. Or maybe some weird root vegetable, like rutabaga or cassava. How can the White House chef be expected to stock everything the President may develop a sudden craving for? My father would say that if he was the White House chef, he would lie awake at night, worrying. I replied that if I were President, I would stick to my pre-planned menu and he could relax. We would work well together.

Time to go to work. I am a theoretical physicist at the National Science Foundation. Science is about asking good questions, about approaching a truth knowing it can never be fully reached. My father loved questions. Maybe he didn't ask the right ones.

I put on my N95 mask. You can't be too careful. I walk to the Woodley Park–Zoo Metro station and take the long escalator down. My favorite Metro station arrival announcement of all time was back in the eighties:

Next stop: Woodley Park–Zoo: home of the longest escalator in the Free World.

Were there longer escalators in Moscow, Havana, Pyongyang? Questions beget questions. Had he lived to see it, my father would have loved talking Metrorail trivia. For example, the chimes that sound when the train doors close—*bing, bong!*—are the first two notes of "Swing Low, Sweet Chariot." And the Metro stations' vaulted ceilings are an excellent example of brutalist architecture. And if you fall on the tracks and the train is bearing down, there's a crawl space on the side under the platform lights, roomy enough to save you.

I'm in the station, waiting. Behind me stand a group of schoolkids, talking and laughing about their teachers. Twelve years ago I saw Ms. Marvin's obituary in the *Washington Post.* A short paragraph: taught sixth grade for thirteen years in Silver Spring, sold real estate for twenty-five years in Northern Virginia, died after a long illness, survived by two nieces in Ohio. No picture. I'd give it a C-minus. *Where is the heartbreak*, I would scrawl in red ink, *where is the tragedy?*

I can see that faint lick of light creeping up the distant rail, getting closer. It's coming. The platform lights blink as the train pulls in. The doors open. I board and find a seat.

And there he is.

My father sits in a seat across the aisle, facing me.

His doppelgänger? He looks the way I remember him: the shiny bald spot, the wrinkly whimsical eyes, the white button-up shirt and blue striped necktie he wore to work. He is sitting next to the priority seating sign. *Federal law requires these seats be reserved for the disabled, the elderly, and the ethereal.* Ha, ha. Our kind of joke. Why would a ghost take public transportation? Did he take the escalator or just float up to the surface through granite and bedrock and dirt? Questions beget questions.

I've long since forgiven him. I no longer lie awake at night, trying to solve the mystery of why he left us on that bright October day. I have my theories. Untreated clinical depression is at the top of the list.

When I was five, he took me to Toys"R"Us, then my favorite place in the world. I ran down the board game aisle, zigged and zagged, then ran down the toy truck aisle. I turned around and my father was gone. I was lost. I stopped crying when they announced my name on the store intercom: *meet your father next to the Rock'em Sock'em Robots.* I knew exactly where to go.

The train is filling up. Standing room only. I can still glimpse him through the crush of people. Our eyes meet. He smiles that sheepish grin and gives me that apologetic shrug of his shoulders.

Bing, bong. The doors close. And he is gone.

Acknowledgments

THANK YOU to all the people who helped me and stood behind me as I wrote this novel. I'm grateful to my long-standing Bethesda "Stromboli's" writing group, who provided much-valued comments and support as I pushed through the first draft. Thank you: Barbara de Boinville, Meredith Eaton, Peter Gorman, Cathy Hostetler, Heather Morton, Jessica Piscitelli Robinson, and Katie Spurlock.

Thanks also to my other two writing groups, who offered terrific feedback on various pieces of the revision. Thanks to Jeremie Amoroso, Aviad Eilam, Leslie Ekstrom, Denise Robbins, Leslie Spitz-Edson, Amy Tercek, and Alexia Underwood. Thanks to B. K. Atrostic, Lyvita Brooks, Judith Goff, Jessica Clare Haney, Andy Harney, Oxana Holtman, Dayle McCarthy, Petra Meindl-Andrews, and Ellen Schofield. And thanks to Kim Tidwell for her very helpful comments on my first chapter.

I'm beyond thankful to the Washington Writers' Publishing House for honoring me with the 2023 WWPH Fiction Prize and providing an awesome array of editorial feedback and support. Thank you Suzanne Feldman, Caroline Bock, Kathleen Wheaton, and Adam Schwartz. Another big thank you to copy editor-extraordinaire Kathleen Mills, whose eagle eye caught so many embarrassing mistakes. Kudos to Andrew Sargus Klein for the cover and to Barbara Shaw for the interior book design.

I want to thank my family. To my mom, Mollee Kruger, who is my inspiration as a writer. To my dad, Jerome Kruger, who passed away in 2013 and is missed every day. And to my brother Joe and all of my in-laws, nieces, and nephews. Love you guys!

And finally, infinite appreciation and love to my talented and wonderful wife, Cynthia Folcarelli, for her invaluable editorial input and unwavering support.

Reading Group Discussion Questions

• What would you say is the central theme of *Bad Questions*? What roles do spirituality, religious belief, and pseudoscience play in the novel?

• Why does Billy feel guilt over his father's suicide and view himself as "the wicked son"? How do his father's actions change Billy's life?

• What are some of the bad questions Billy and his father ask in *Bad Questions*?

• How does Billy's relationship with his father compare and contrast with his relationship with his mother?

• What roles do Judaism and Jewish themes play in *Bad Questions*?

• One of Billy's main challenges is moving to a new city and adjusting to a new school in the midst of adolescence. Did your family move when you were growing up? How did your experience in a new school compare with Billy's?

• Throughout *Bad Questions*, Billy relies on late 1960s and early '70s pop culture (e.g., television shows, *Mad Magazine*, the Washington Senators baseball team) to help him make sense of the world. When you were Billy's age, which pop culture items or moments were particularly influential in your life?

• *Bad Questions* takes place in 1971. How do you think Billy's story would be different if it had taken place in the present day? For example, how would social media or the internet have affected his experience?

More from the Washington Writers' Publishing House

You Cannot Save Here
Tonee (Anthony) Moll

The Witch Bottle & Other Stories
Suzanne Feldman

Why I Cannot Take a Lover
Grace Cavalieri

Altamira
Myra Sklarew

Washington Writers' Publishing House

Washington Writers' Publishing House (WWPH) is an independent, nonprofit, cooperative press founded in 1975. Our mission is to publish and celebrate writers from DC, Maryland, and Virginia. To learn more about our fiction, poetry, and creative nonfiction manuscript contests, our bi-weekly literary journal, *WWPH Writes*, and to purchase more WWPH books, please visit:

www.washingtonwriters.org

Follow us on:
Twitter: @wwphpress
Facebook: @WWPH
Instagram: @writingfromWWPH

Contact us at:
wwphpress@gmail.com

Sign up for our bi-weekly, online literary journal, *WWPH Writes*, by scanning the QR Code on the right. Free to subscribe and free to submit. Emails are only twice a month. Be part of the Washington Writers' Publishing House community, the (almost) 50-year-old cooperative, nonprofit literary press based in our nation's capital.

CPSIA information can be obtained
at www.ICGtesting.com
Printed in the USA
BVHW040456260723
667774BV00001B/4